Pretend I'm Not Here

Stories

Trey Sager

ISBN: 978-1-942004-94-3

Library of Congress Control Number: 2026937867

Cover art by Paul Chan

ELJ Editions, Ltd.
P.O. Box 815
Washingtonville, NY 10992

www.elj-editions.com

Trey Sager's stories illuminate people who prefer shadows. His beautifully written, very compelling stories engage the reader in characters whose interior lives are at odds with their place in the world. They doubt and have no idea they have a place in it. Sager's take on friendships and family recognize hurt and alienation, where life is always puzzling. His stories disdain the obvious for the intriguing, subtle, and intelligent. Sometimes perverse and never sentimental, Trey Sager's debut collection welcomes a wonderful, unusual writer.

—Lynne Tillman, author of *Men and Apparitions* and *Paying Attention*

Trey Sager explores the dark places of our cities and souls. He shows us fractured families and psyches, desperate eroticism, and the technological dystopias of the immediate future. *Pretend I'm Not Here* is an ambitious, funny, and violently prophetic book. It's the best collection of short stories I've read in years.

—Rav Grewal-Kök, author of *The Snares*

These stories start out in familiar territories, realisms invoking people and places around America, until they flatly reveal they are more unfamiliar, weirder, wrong-er, sexier, and sometimes more terrifying and sad, and more speculative, than what it seemed they were going to be doing. But then you've got to realize that they got more real—more accurate. I became interested in that motion each of these stories made, and ever impacted by Sager's decisive vision on the discrete plane of the sentence, where a camera has a "snout" and a pair of white lace underwear wraps around a perverted aristocrat's ankle, in a ritualistic tryst with a robot, "like a manacle."

—Caren Beilin, author of *Sea, Poison* and *Revenge of the Scapegoat*

Trey Sager's fiction is the future this reader wants. Tender and brutal, perfect for lovers of David Lynch, Sager's sentences take hold and keep you in their grip.

—Kathleen Heil, author of *You Can Have It All*

Table of Contents

Love Calls You by Your Name

I got to the producer's house around nine. It looked dark inside, and was much too hot for a cocktail party. I'd left my pills in the glove compartment, in a gold case I'd bought at a vintage shop a long time ago, back when dosing myself seemed a little more glamorous, and I thought of running back to the car, driving up Mulholland and diminishing my relationship to the world. But I soldiered on because, in between shoots and on the radio, everyone had been complaining about the locusts up there, the locusts were the talk of the town, and honestly it sounded a little terrifying. They'd come two years early and at night they feasted on chaparral and telephone wires or whatever. Lionel said it was all the proof we needed—of what I had no idea.

I plucked a flute of champagne from a catering tray. I don't like to drink but it's the kind of thing you do if you want to keep eating lunch in this town. A few people were swishing through the hallway, laughing and touching each other's hands. One of them complimented my dress and said she'd admired it at a party earlier that spring. I tried to remember a mistake she'd made, even something insignificant—she had a tattoo of cherry blossoms on her forearm and you couldn't see it very well because her skin was so tan. That's the best I could come up with.

"Thank you," I said.

At the end of the hall, I passed a shelf of gold trophies notable because they weren't Emmys, and from there I found my way to the living room, a lofty space with a high, sloped ceiling made of glass. Dark palms rose from terracotta pots and the cast and crew members mingled throughout the room. After years of working together, their faces were so familiar they'd become the cabinet spices I ignored when looking for the cumin, the only one I ever seemed to use.

"Helen," a voice said behind me.

It was Agnes.

"Am I allowed to talk about it? Can we talk about Hong Kong?" she asked, as if the producers—or maybe I?—had banned the topic from conversation.

"Yes," I said. "Of course."

"It's terrible, isn't it? But what's going on?"

She was sweating. Not a lot, but she had a definite glaze. Her bamboo pattern dress swamped her waist but the top opened as elegantly as a calla lily, and her hair drizzled onto her shoulders like Spanish moss. For a moment, it seemed as if she was not really Agnes at all, she was some equatorial fertility goddess.

"The government is in crisis," I said. "They won't let anyone leave."

"The people are really suffering."

"That's Buddhism for you," I said dismissively, trying to invoke one of the four noble truths but instead sounding vaguely racist.

"Well, it's unimaginable," she said, taking a quick drink from a glass of beer.

Agnes had always struck me as vapid. Which, to be honest, is not the worst quality in an actress. It's up there with narcissistic and insecure. You might expect those behaviors to torpedo a career, but they can make the difference between a callback and a long dark night of journaling. Vapid didn't bother me. What annoyed me about Agnes was all her evangelizing about the benefits of Jojoba oil, which she apparently rubbed onto her skin after every shower, and her TMI reports about her barely legal boyfriend. And, at some point, she'd developed enough clout to establish a rule—if you had a scene with her that day, you had to meet her for breakfast and review lines, which is when I discovered her revolting habit of putting maple syrup in her coffee.

"Don't you just love a good party?" she asked. Her lips curled into a smile, and she looked more like herself.

"A good one, yes," I said.

"Oh, Helen. I really wish you'd stop it," she said.

"Stop what?" I asked innocently.

"Going rogue," she said, rolling her eyes. She was about to go on when

Cyrus, the hair and makeup artist, wedged between us, accompanied on his upper lip by what was surely a leading candidate for cold sore of the year. He lassoed his arm around Agnes's waist—how did such an enormous man ever get *that* job, I wondered—and hauled her over to a pair of skeletal production assistants. As if working from a secret script, they all dipped their heads and laughed.

I lingered for another hour, just long enough, I hoped, to ensure I'd be in everyone's recollection. Before I left, I saw Lionel. I could tell he was reveling in some delicious secret just by the way he dredged the syllables of my name. Of course I was curious, but not enough to stick around, especially after one of the minor characters, who'd been killed off in the previous episode, came over and made a joke about rising from the dead to get his revenge. I found it a little pathetic. Lionel had the kindness to smile.

The next morning, I made a couple of seven-minute eggs. Honestly I prefer a fried egg. The sizzle of a frying pan has a certain appeal to an American actress. In our coterie, there's the archetype of a woman patrolling the aisles of a diner with a pot of hot coffee, dressed in a dusky pink uniform and serving solemn men in flannel shirts. The reality is, though, I don't need the grease. What I *do* need is a slightly runny yolk and protein. A seven-minute egg is a good compromise. To keep them from exploding you just have to run them under the tap first.

I sat down in front of the television and found *Dry Ice* on demand. "A serial killer and his family meet life's everyday challenges head on—and the heads start rolling." Lionel—his character's name was also Lionel—works at a dry ice manufacturer and packages his victims in dry ice before shipping them to a friend's warehouse, where the bodies are conveniently dissolved in enormous tubs of acid. So, *Dry Ice*. Part comedy, part soap opera. The show does nothing to explore Lionel's motivations—there isn't even a glib backstory of child abuse—but in Los Angeles literally every movie advertisement has a gun on it, so it seems like maybe the world's OK with some casual unexamined violence.

Agnes plays Charlotte, Lionel's wife. I'm Vivian, the susceptible neighbor. I fast-forwarded to one of our scenes, where Charlotte and Vivian meet at their children's school because the teacher has disappeared—Lionel garroted him—and Vivian wants to discuss how the kids are coping.

"Ever since Jack left, the kids…they've really been acting out," Vivian says.

"Maybe Lionel can talk to them," Charlotte says encouragingly. "Maybe they need a man to set them straight."

"No, no, I don't think that's such a good idea," Vivian says.

"Why not?" Charlotte acts surprised.

"I'm sorry," Vivian says. "I have to ask, is everything OK at home?"

Charlotte stares at Vivian suspiciously.

"What makes you ask?" she says.

"Well," Vivian says, "I had insomnia last night, so I made myself a cup of peppermint tea. I was drinking it by the front window and happened to see Lionel outside."

"Oh?" Charlotte asks, her eyes widening.

"Yes," Vivian says. "He was…prowling through the shadows. It looked like he was dragging something heavy."

"Are you sure it was him?"

Charlotte takes Vivian's hand.

Here, the writers wanted Charlotte to suggest that I'd seen someone else—a sex offender who'd just broken out of prison—and that the steam from the tea had fogged the window. I was supposed to make light of how thank god I wasn't raped.

As Charlotte begins to speak, Vivian reaches for her and strokes her cheek.

"No," Vivian says. "I know what I saw."

"What, what are you, what are you doing?" Charlotte stammers.

She shifts uncomfortably on her feet, feeling for a wall that isn't there as Vivian leans in slowly. The two women look at each other, then Vivian kisses Charlotte on the lips. They bow their heads like lovers weary with grief.

"I know," Vivian says.

Going rogue, Agnes had called it. Improvising. That had been the first time. Paul, the director, never told me to stop. On shoot days he treated me like a shaman. I tried to be professional about it because I found Agnes so vulgar—everything she did seemed to ooze—and yet Charlotte, with the same raw materials, had cast a spell. There was tension in our storyline—I don't know how the writers missed it—with me living next door all lonely and lost and Charlotte desperate to escape the prison of her complicity. So I took the initiative, which wasn't like me at all, and it wasn't very Vivian either, but it felt right.

The phone rang.

"You left early," Lionel said.

"God has a script for all of us," I said.

"Funny you should say that," he snickered. "Are you free tonight?"

"I don't need another ambush, Lionel."

"How many times do I have to apologize?"

"Many, many more times."

"My stars, Helen. He was not a bad person."

"No, but he was a bald person."

"I'm not setting you up this time. I promise. Seven o'clock?"

"Get cigarettes," I said.

I straightened up the apartment, mostly escorting magazines from one room to another. After a late afternoon shower, I drove to Valley Vino for two bottles of red, then stopped at Gelson's, where I bought a tin of overpriced Marcona almonds. While walking past the butcher, I was surprised to see so many people in line. Apparently there was a special on pigeon.

In the parking lot, a woman dressed in black kneeled to tie her sneaker. Next to her, an old man in a cowboy hat clapped sarcastically. Were they related? I sensed that the woman was not really tying her shoe, she was trying to avoid the man, and for a second I thought of offering her a ride. I pulled out of my spot but when I looked in the rearview mirror, the woman was gone. The man was still there clapping.

Lionel lived way up in the hills. He said he needed a certain amount of distance from other people, which didn't make him special, it just made him rich. A wooden gate shielded the driveway from his neighbors. On the inside, stone bodhisattvas presided over abundant flowers. The house itself was a gleaming white cube with tinted black windows. It'd served as a refuge for me many times. When the gate opened and I saw Lionel standing barefoot on the grass, a butterfly on his finger, I found my heart smothered in gratitude.

"Aren't you a sight for sore eyes," I said.

We kissed hello. His breath smelled freshly masked.

"Come around back," he smiled.

On a glass dining table next to the pool, Lionel had laid out a feast. Casually he ticked off the menu items—dandelion greens tossed with lemon juice, caramelized beets, a fennel raita and two steaming pigeon pies, which I should've seen coming. A loose gold bracelet dripped from his wrist as he splashed wine into our goblets. I found myself staring at his marvelous black chest hair through his unbuttoned shirt.

Right away he launched into a tasty bit of gossip. He spent a great deal of time on set, much more than I did, so through his stories I could judge everyone without actually having to know them. We often discussed the best way to murder everyone on the cast and crew. It seemed like a natural thing to do. For Agnes, we agreed on poison. For Paul, our director, a decisive gunshot to the temple. For Cyrus, I suggested a staged autoerotic asphyxiation. I really wanted to humiliate Cyrus. I was angry that he believed himself beautiful. I know beauty is relative, eye of the beholder and all that, but if I had to half starve for it, and someone like Cyrus was also beautiful, then the word just didn't mean anything.

Lionel said one of the production assistants, whose job seemed to be getting out of people's way, was dating Paul's son. By accident she mixed up her texts and sent a dirty one to Paul.

"What did he do?" I asked.

"He went to her apartment. He didn't know she was dating his son. Paul thought he was getting a blowjob."

"Oh my god," I snorted.

Lionel slid a wedge of pigeon pie in front of me. He was usually an excellent cook but I found the pastry tough, and the caramelized beets more burnt than candied. Probably for the best, I thought, heaping more greens onto my plate.

"Have you ever stayed at the Chelsea Hotel?" he asked.

"In New York?" I asked. "I thought they tore it down."

Lionel shook his head. "It's under construction, but they still keep a few floors open for people like us."

I must've looked puzzled because, exasperated, he said, "*Celebrities*."

"Anyway," he continued, "I was there last week to shoot a commercial. After we wrapped, I had a gentleman caller over and was doing my melancholy man at the window routine when I saw the most remarkable thing. It looked like a small tornado of seeds churning above the traffic outside. There were thousands of them. But they weren't moving in a circle, they were all scribbling around in different directions, yet they stayed more or less contained inside the shape of a funnel."

"What were they?"

"Bees! I couldn't tell at first but the tornado came closer and closer. They began to settle on a tree branch right outside my window. I mean, there were thousands of them knotted there together."

"Sounds Biblical."

"Exactly! That's exactly right. They were building a nest. Unfortunately, my friend didn't care. After a few hours, I went back to the window, but the bees had vanished. The branch was as bare as my arm."

As if on cue, a pair of rabbits poked their heads out from the bamboo stalks surrounding the pool. One hobbled over to the water's edge and began to drink.

"I read last year that cell phones were the reason all the bees were dying. Did you hear that?"

Lionel shook his head. I wasn't sure he'd heard me.

"Anyway," he said, turning back toward me and refilling my glass, "You're going to want to drink this."

"No, thanks, I—"

"Helen, I'm leaving the show."

If you're an aging television actress, you need three things—coping mechanisms, survival strategies and friends. I took a pill sometimes and I did a lot of Pilates. Like, *a lot* of Pilates—my heart was probably decrepit but my core could pit an olive. As for friends, Lionel was the closest thing I had, though I trusted him only to a point. Maybe it was because we could never be lovers. Or maybe because actors are always performing and can't tell what's real. Or maybe because Lionel was so much bigger than this town and I was just getting the most out of what I had, lucky to be here, who would've thunk it, Helen from Ohio. Even so, I had no one else, and without Lionel, it was only a matter of time before everyone looked at me like I was some shriveled up eggplant leeching off the vine.

"I've already discussed terms with Stanley and Mitchel," he continued. "They're talking to the writers now to find a graceful exit."

"Why on earth would they let you leave?"

"Actually, it was their idea," he said. "And it's working out. I landed a movie deal and we film in Ibiza next month."

"There's no show without you," I said, indignant.

"I'm flattered, Helen. But don't make me do one of those eye rolls where I see my brain and have a stroke."

"What?"

"It's not my show anymore. It's yours. And Agnes's, I guess. The network is having a grand mal orgasm because of you. They think you've tapped into something big and fresh."

"Oh, for fuck's sake."

I drank the wine, leaned back and looked up at the night sky.

"Did you get the cigarettes?" I asked.

He fished a box of Nat Shermans from his pocket—the flavorless neon ones. Sometimes his garish tastes got the better of him. I lit one and breathed in the punishing smoke, and thought momentarily of those black and white images of Marlene Dietrich holding a cigarette, black velvet, silver and snow.

"Aren't you happy? Isn't it what you want? You've got the lead," Lionel said.

"I haven't thought about what I've wanted in years."

"Then you must be a true artist."

"No, I'm a fool, and you're a monster for having a laugh at me."

"Oh, tut tut."

"What are you accusing me of, exactly? Just so I understand."

"Well, either you've been angling for the lead and your improvisations aren't improvisations at all, they're calculated—in which case, congratulations—or you're genuinely channeling your character, which is what all of us dream of doing, although I haven't believed in that idea in twenty-five years, but either way, it'd appear that I'm jealous."

I took a long drag.

"Why did you become an actor?"

"Oh, here we go. Spare me, Helen."

"To become another person, of course," I said. "But it feels a little less magical when you start doing paper towel commercials and the other person you're becoming is a housewife obsessed with countertops. For a while I just wanted to scrape enough money to go to some remote island where I didn't have to talk to anyone or be anything for as long as possible. Actually, I still want that. But even then, it's an act. You're not really there. You're just performing the tourist. It's all an act."

Lionel scratched his nose, looking a little embarrassed and a little angry.

"But why now?" Lionel asked. "You've been playing Vivian for three and a half seasons."

"I don't know," I said. "It came out of the story. Vivian tells me what she—"

"Vivian is a character," he said. "She's a costume you put on."

"I don't mean it literally. Anyway, I thought you'd be happy that I took charge."

"But you're not. You're being so passive about it. You're blaming her."

I felt the flush of wine in my cheeks and fingertips. Half my cigarette had turned to ash. I tapped it, took another drag and closed my eyes. The dishes clattered around me, then the door to the house swung open and closed. I listened to the first locusts scratch up the night.

After a few moments, I followed Lionel inside.

On a long wooden table next to the kitchen, Lionel had piled up murder props from the show—there was the crowbar he'd used to bludgeon the mayor, an old heretic's fork he made himself, and the bellows he'd shoved into his mother's mouth and pumped until her lungs exploded. On the back wall, I noticed that he'd replaced one of his paintings with an original Francis

Bacon. A face full of butchered meat spluttered from the collar of a suit. The background was bright orange.

Lionel had always been cynical but I'd never been the target. Now that I'd betrayed our shared negativity, he was angry. But it wasn't my fault. It just happened. I'd begun to notice Charlotte during scenes, or Vivian did, rather, her lips, her skin, her inner frenzy. She was different than Agnes, less cloying, too short to be called voluptuous, though I suppose they were the same size. Charlotte summoned something inside me when I was Vivian, and in some desperate and elemental way, I was drawn to her. I couldn't stop thinking of her, the two of us entangled, and felt something unusual like hope.

"Let's go to a party," Lionel said. "It'll be a good one."

There was always a party.

"You sure?"

"Actually, give me a few minutes to think it over," he said sarcastically.

He went to the bedroom to shower. I sagged onto the couch and called my sister—no answer, not unusual—then scrolled the *New York Times*. I found an article about Taiwan and the Solomon Islands, and how foreign governments call Taiwan another name whenever they're speaking with China—it was about "the linguistics of sovereignty" or something like that. It got me thinking about the Falkland Islands, and the war there in the early eighties. I couldn't remember who'd won. I could still see the drab colors of the land behind the televised soldiers, and I wondered who they belonged to.

Lionel came out in a red silk shirt and white jeans. I looked at my dress. It was black, more of a cloaking device.

"Is this appropriate?" I asked.

"It'll do," he said.

I hadn't realized how airtight his house was until we walked outside. The locusts sounded like knives falling through sheets of glass. I thought of the nervous women in horror movies who never make it to their cars. I reached for Lionel's arm. He stiffened as we walked. Safely inside the car, with the doors shut and the engine on, I could still hear them.

We drove by boxy houses teetering on beams and stucco dwellings overrun with jungle plants. Occasionally through the trees I could glimpse the sprawl below, a vast grid of glowing yellow embers.

"What's the party all about?" I asked.

"It's for a friend of mine. I think you've met her. Fiona, from Mexico City."

"The astrologer?"

"It's her birthday."

"Do Libras make good astrologers?"

"What do you know about the zodiac?"

We arrived around ten. I followed Lionel into a grisly looking building with yellow cursive letters affixed to the outside: "Murder Bar." Apparently in the thirties a struggling actress had strangled her bichon frisé there. Inside, everything was covered in red cellophane. Lionel barked into my ear but I couldn't make out the words, the music was too loud, and he capered off to the bathroom with a man who had long straight white hair.

I thought of running out. I could call a car and be home by eleven. But I had no other claim for my attention, only the depressing prospect of watching television, so I went to the bar and asked for the house red.

A warm hand seized my arm. It was Fiona. Her dress looked like it was made of bubbles. I'd only met her once before, at Lionel's, when she asked all the guests to select a card from her tarot deck. I'd picked the Tower and she'd acted strangely affectionate toward me ever since. After I wished her a happy birthday, she smiled anxiously at me, as if I hadn't finished my line.

"You look gorgeous," I added, lifting my palms like why do we even try. I scanned her face for signs of aging—there were none, but she was on the edge of some anxiety, I could tell.

"Oh, you're so sweet. I'm glad you came, Helen."

"Me too," I said.

"I love what you're doing on the show," she said, dipping her shoulder. "I could see it coming that day at the pool. I mean, all my clients want someone to wag a finger at them and tell them what to do, but sometimes, I tell them, destiny is a selfie you don't recognize—you have hands, use them."

I didn't quite follow her. Probably she'd had a few drinks. It was her birthday after all. So I smiled and said, "When I want someone to wag their finger, I come right out and ask."

"Oh, Helen. You're very funny. I see why Lionel's so fond of you."

I waited for her to excuse herself, maybe glance over at the door and see someone she just had to say hello to. People were always searching for a way out. But Fiona stood there waiting expectantly.

"Well, he adores you," I managed.

"If they didn't need guidance, I wouldn't have a job," she said.

"Who?"

"My clients."

"Oh," I said. "Like a bar needs alcoholics."

She leaned back and laughed. The bartender gave me a low look. Was he listening? I heard the song for the first time, it was the song about putting on a clown face, the one I always shut off in the car, absolutely not.

"It's your birthday. Can I buy you a drink?" I asked, thinking that's what people do.

Fiona pointed her finger at me, tsk tsk, or come with me, I wasn't sure, and she whispered in my ear, "You really are something else," before walking to the dance floor. Her friends gathered around. They looked happy. She looked happy. She looked over in my direction, smiled and flung her arms into the air.

I've always felt like a bathroom says a lot about a bar or restaurant. It's where the owners are more daring in their personality or sense of humor, where they can inflict some kind of experience on you. Maybe it's because the person inside the bathroom is trapped, they go in alone to relieve themselves, it's a vulnerable place. Of course there are plenty of cookie cutter facilities with egg-shaped sinks and walnut paneling, but those show a lack of aspiration, a desire to be acceptably bourgeois—I'm talking about places that have artisanal cowgirl pornography on the wall or video art of women burning in special effect flames.

I expected Murder Bar would feature a salon of starlet headshots. Something like that. You'd have to puzzle together their connection. Lots of no-name teenagers along with Janet Leigh and Angie Dickinson. Women murdered on film. Women whose role was to die. But after a long wait in line, I found the walls bare. Their color was pale orange, and an odorless prayer candle burned on the upper basin of the toilet. In the mirror, I was the only starlet.

I tried to tease out my hair a bit, it'd gotten a little clumped at the top, and a strange question came to me, do corpses get bedhead? Is that something morticians need to account for? That would've been a better job for Cyrus, by the way. To doll up the dead. Yes, of course, I guessed, but did I look like a corpse, to ask such a thing? Too much makeup? The light was a florescent bar on the ceiling. It didn't help. I peered into the mirror, and thought I looked more like Vivian than me, the way my hair spumed from the center part and over my shoulders like a suburban orgasm. I imagined her inside the mirror, staring back at me, the actress who played her, evaluating my makeup—what a perfect word for all that it accomplished—and what it hid, a face caressed again and again by the hands of a clock.

"Go," she whispered.

I pushed my way through the crowded bar. Fiona was still dancing beautifully. Lionel was nowhere to be seen.

In the taxi home, I started a mental to-do list. But I got anxious thinking about Monday. It hit me that I wasn't ready for this next stage. Lionel leaving the show was too steep a price to pay for some simple improvisations. I'd been so defensive when talking to him. I'd clung to my cover story, which I hadn't realized was a cover story—because the story underneath was much more oblique. Maybe I'd blamed Vivian because I was ashamed of my attraction to Charlotte, humid, arms joggling whenever she thrust across a room. Our kiss was a chaos. So maybe it wasn't Vivian, maybe it was me, and so what then? What did that say about Agnes, who I found intolerable? Was it only lust?

What even was a person, a body or a story?

On Monday morning, I drove to the diner to meet her. I found her in a booth next to a window. If I had to bet yes or no as to whether she'd brushed her hair, and my life depended on it, it was basically a coin flip. She could get away with things like that, the wild and unconquerable Agnes.

"Helen," she said, drawing out the last letter. "I love the oversized buttons on that jacket. Very Audrey Hepburn."

"I was going for Katharine," I said. "Good weekend?"

"Marvelous," she smiled, arching her eyebrows suggestively. "Victor and I never got out of bed."

The waitress came over. She had an awful lot of blonde hair. I asked for egg whites and multigrain toast, no butter. Yolks were weekends only. Agnes already had her plate of food and was chopping her pancakes into small bites.

When I took my script out and laid it on the table, she laughed, "Why even bother with *that*?"

But she put on her reading glasses and we started to rehearse.

The scene began with Vivian and Charlotte on the front lawn. The neighbor across the street had been hosting parties over the weekends, and we'd both witnessed SUVs full of girls in tinsel dresses arrive with gruesome-looking men.

"What do you think they do in there?" Vivian asks, gesturing toward the house.

"Well, they're not playing Monopoly," Charlotte says. "I wonder if we should send Lionel over to take a look."

She arches her eyebrow, probing Vivian's reaction—does Vivian understand the veiled threat?

"I feel bad for those girls," Vivian says.

Charlotte says again, "Let's ask Lionel to go over there."

"What if we confront the neighbor instead?" I suggested.

Agnes bit off a sharp look, then said, "That'd change the whole episode. If Lionel doesn't go over there, he won't kill him in the second act..."

"The man-protector thing is sort of silly though," I said.

"Helen, we haven't been here two minutes and you're already trying to change the script. Let the writers write. Let the actors act."

"But what if we went to the door together?" I asked again, reaching for something, the salt or her hand.

"Why do you insist on doing this?" she said, slapping the table. Her fork clattered. A few people turned toward us, then looked away. "It's ridiculous. You probably want us to take off each other's clothes and then knock on the neighbor's door and slash his throat."

"I thought maybe if we talked about it beforehand, it'd be better. If you were more involved. Instead of surprising you during the scene."

"Aren't they improvisations?"

"Yes, but…"

She stabbed a bit of pancake. I watched her chew and swallow. A few morsels clung to her lips. She ate like a young girl who hadn't learned to hate herself.

"You know what you need? You need to get laid," she said.

The waitress came over and slid a plate in front of me. I looked over at Agnes, who covered the rest of her pancakes with a napkin. She drank from her mug of coffee. Her skin looked warm. All her rings were silver. I didn't know anymore about Vivian or Charlotte, or Agnes or Helen. I felt the slowness of my breath, the up and down of it, in my chest, and I heard murmurs from different parts of the room, and I sensed my eyes beginning to tear. This person sitting across from me was someone I despised and someone I desired, and I didn't want her to be Agnes anymore, and I didn't want to be Helen, I didn't want her as myself, I didn't want to be loved for who I was, I just wanted to be swept away, I wanted to be erased.

She placed a crisp twenty-dollar bill next to her plate, rose from the table and left.

I sat and ate my egg whites. Afterward, I paid the check and went outside. A couple of old men in wheelchairs were parked on the curb, watching traffic. I asked if one of them had a cigarette.

"Well," one said.

"How about you," the other said.

"You're right there, aren't you," the first one said.

"Do you have a cigarette?" I asked again.

They turned back to the traffic.

I drove to the studio, which was only five minutes away. I hadn't had enough coffee so I stopped at the cart. The same man—Alex—was there every day. He handed me a hot Styrofoam cup and smiled. It boggled my mind that we still used Styrofoam. The ocean had a plastic island the size of Texas and we weren't doing anything about it.

"Thanks, Alex."

I turned to go but he waved at me.

"My name is not really Alex," he said.

"No?"

"It's Roberto," he said.

"Oh. Why do we all call you Alex?" I asked.

"The last man was Alex."

I told him I was sorry, though he didn't seem to care that much, just enough to report the error. I told him I'd tell the others, but probably wouldn't—my stock would rise when everyone kept calling him Alex and he'd think I was the only one who respected him enough to use his real name.

It was still very early. The studio was dark and quiet. Near the equipment room I saw David, the cinematographer, talking to a woman from the network. He had on one of those tweed caps and was straddling a stool, and she wore a gray pantsuit and heels—I don't actually know if she was from the network but that's the kind of thing an executive would wear to the set. She touched his shoulder and laughed as I passed by, and I guessed that they were sleeping together.

On my dressing room door someone had affixed a sticky note with nothing written on it. I went inside and found a terrible mess. I don't know what it was about protein bars but they seemed to exert some mysterious power that prevented me from ever throwing out the wrappers. On the vanity, I'd left uncapped tubes of ointment and several blotting tissues. Clothes were draped over the chair. Torn cardboard boxes on the floor. Piles of papers, mail, magazines.

When I was younger, everyone took dating so seriously. And there was an expectation of progress. When a relationship failed, it was supposed to teach you something that helped you later on. Everyone seemed to be striving for the same endgame. I guess marriage. But I never knew what I was doing. I never really learned anything. I grew weary of men and their elaborate idiotic attempts to fuck me. I'd never been with a woman—I didn't hate the idea, but I didn't love it either. I just didn't really care. If I'd dated women, would that have made life any easier? All my relationships failed because they'd been with actual people, and actual people are the most insincere performances. I'd tried to be a woman—a person people thought of when they thought of what a woman was—and I'd tried to be beautiful, I'd tried to be successful, but they weren't my ideas, I just propped them up along with everyone else, we all just forced each other to assimilate to these things that lived between us and no one actually wanted.

Call time was eleven. I drank my coffee. After slipping into Vivian's usual gray cashmere V-neck and blue jeans, I went out to find Cyrus so he could fix my makeup, but he was blow-drying Agnes's hair. A few sycophants stood next to her, watching her hair billow. Agnes glanced my way. When she saw me, she pretended to smile. It was too loud to say anything because of the hair dryer so I just stood there. Finally, Cyrus shut it off, and with his hand he motioned me into the chair even though Agnes's ends were still wet.

We did the scene the way it was written. Agnes sent Lionel to the neighbor's house and he eviscerated the man with a pair of scissors. There wasn't much chatter on set. Everyone was all business. Paul didn't say anything to me about the scene. Neither did Lionel. At six o'clock, we wrapped, and I didn't change, I just went straight for my car and took a pill. I couldn't go home. I couldn't face the emptiness of my apartment and prepare some miserable dinner. I felt sick, like I'd just put an animal to sleep. So I decided to go for a drive.

The sun went down as I made my way to Burbank. I saw the dusty orange sky in the rearview mirror, and ahead, the night was coming on. It wasn't long before the mountains behind Burbank blended in. There were fewer cars out than usual, and almost no one on the sidewalk. Before turning onto Crystal Springs, I took another pill, why not, then drifted through Griffith Park. I considered stopping at the old Greek Theatre if it were empty, but for what purpose, I asked myself, what good would that do.

I passed through Los Feliz and Silver Lake. By then the lights from the cars and buildings were beginning to blur and I wasn't sure if I should continue. I remembered Agnes lived in Los Feliz and found myself turning around. Her Spanish style house was set off the road on a steep hill. The baby cypress trees on the lawn weren't tall enough to hide the windows and I could see Agnes, or her silhouetted figure, fussing about the second floor, maybe searching for her keys or phone.

I slid down into my seat. I remembered I had a cigarette after all, one I'd taken from Lionel the other night, a neon green one, and lit it. The car was still running. I could feel the husky rattle of the engine in my legs. It wasn't a powerful car. It wasn't smooth either. The streetlights were bright as heaven. I watched Agnes throw her arms into the air. A dance or exasperation. I couldn't tell. I moved my hand between my legs and rubbed my palm there. I let the cigarette burn in the ashtray. The locusts screeched all around me. Agnes leaned against a wall. I slipped my fingers underneath the waistband of my jeans. She just stood there. I don't think she was doing anything. Maybe listening to music. I came. I barely had to move.

Time passed. I might've dozed off. I don't know. A sharp knock on my window startled me. Agnes was peering in, her hand against her forehead like a woman staring into fog.

"What are you doing here?" she asked accusingly.

I'd always admired the softness in her eyes. She was angry but it was a rounded, hospitable anger, something you could work with. It's what made Charlotte so sympathetic. It didn't occur to me to say anything. I didn't even roll down the window. I picked up the cigarette and the ash crumbled off the unlit filter, then looked up at the house, the figure was still in the window, then back at Agnes.

"Do you want to come inside?" she asked.

Her living room was hung with black and white photographs taken in Central America, Africa and Asia. Agnes was always at the center, surrounded by local women. They wrapped their arms around her. There was an abundance of cloth. And teeth. So many smiles.

She led me to the couch. Her boyfriend stood beside her. He was so young and beautiful. A personal trainer, I think. Victor. Short. Maybe Peruvian. In a sleeveless tee and gym shorts. I didn't see a television. I reached for Agnes's hand and she let me take it. It was so warm. I wondered if she still had the burden of her parents. Victor left the room and returned with a glass of water for me.

"You can stay here tonight," she said.

"Do you want coffee?" the boyfriend asked.

I shook my head.

They left the room. I heard them whispering. Then Victor returned.

"OK, up you go," he said, lifting me in his arms and laying me on a bed in another room that smelled like a meadow.

Agnes came into the room and she crawled into bed and covered us with the sheets. I felt her full weight next to me, her warm body against mine. She draped her hand over my hip and I felt her breath, the warmth of its arrival, the chill of it leaving, on the back of my neck.

"I'll stay with you tonight," she said. "I'll stay with you just for tonight."

Submit or Surrender

By the time I arrived, Third Avenue was clotted with protesters. Helicopters were chopping up the air. I came to find you, I was sure you'd be there, and I tried to cross the avenue, but the crowd heaved forward and swept me up in their performance of rage. For ten or fifteen blocks I marched with them over the white petals of dogwood trees, which resembled little parachutes. I looked for a way to escape, cursing myself for not coming earlier, but there was no way out. Mounted policemen with washed-out eyes scanned the demonstration from behind metal barricades. The iconic photograph of the protester stuffing a carnation into a rifle came to mind and I realized things had changed so much since then, that the police would kill everyone in the crowd if they got the chance. Next to me, a white man who looked like a Viking in a red raincoat punched the air. His hand was covered in cat scratches. A Dominican couple in matching Moncler coats traded a heavy Ziploc bag of Goldfish back and forth. I thought of that species of blind fish living in underground lakes, and how they'd evolved to not have eyes. A hundred feet away, a woman jabbed her poster into the air—it said "I never met a bomb I didn't love," next to a drawing of a politician masturbating a missile between his legs. The woman wore a black leather motorcycle jacket over a white embroidered dress—I thought it might be you, stumping forward like a confident beast, your hair a beautiful catastrophe. I squeezed through the bodies but when I got close enough you turned toward me, and I saw your eyes sag like melting clocks above a chin jutted low like a spade. I thought maybe you belonged to a church group.

Not you, the person who looked like you.

Nearly everyone at the protest carried a sign.

"If war is the answer, then ask a different question."

"Those who forget history are condemned to repeat it."

I wondered, what if their messages were their dying words, and I sneered at the one about history. The message itself was a repetition. I imagined all the people who had written that quote on their signs and displayed it now, or who'd held that sign in the past—all of them were variations on what they perceived as an unimpeachable truth, but the truth was that the sign always failed. They were condemned not just to repeat it, but also to resemble one another. Of course, I wasn't any different. I was a doppelganger of other doppelgangers, other captives, whose hearts overflowed, speechless at death, lost in the anguish of a pointillist tide.

Limestone buildings ran along the avenue. Net-like stains on the pale facades fossilized in the sunlight. Yesterday's rain had done nothing to wash them away. People pressed their faces against the upper windows. Their sympathies were hard to read—from where I walked even the children had the faces of mannequins. Some actually were mannequins. On the sidewalk, people paused before ducking inside the refuge of a pizzeria. A white teenager in an acid-wash denim jacket briefly joined us, stomping in an exaggerated manner and shouting, but he was only vamping for his friends, who received him back on the curb with a tousle.

I didn't grow up in the city. When I was that boy's age, or maybe a few years younger, I often went to the woods near my house with an imitation rifle. An M-1 carbine. I bought it with my own money that I earned delivering the paper after school. It felt so satisfying to slide the black bolt in and out of the chamber. The heavy wood gave the gun authenticity. But I left it outside so many times that the rain dried out the stock. The wood turned gray like an old fence post. The black metal rusted.

There was a hillock in the woods where I hid photographs that I'd torn out of issues of *Newsweek* and *Time*. The photos were of the war in Lebanon, filled with enormous plumes of charcoal smoke, rubble tumbling out of chalky ruins, boys hurling bottles stuffed with rags and kerosene—exotic indecipherable destruction with overwhelming shapes and colors. I kept the photos under a log and sifted through them whenever I came.

One bright afternoon, after a week of heavy rain, I found them soaked and stuck together. They moldered in my hands when I tried to separate the pages. I don't know what possessed me but I undressed, I'd never done that before, and smeared my face and chest with the remains. The green of the forest and the glare of the sun fell around me like a gown, and I surrendered to it. The birds disappeared, the brush, everything fell away. But then it all came rushing back—I could only get rid of it for just a few seconds.

Beyond the trees, there was an abandoned gravel yard, where massive tires with thick, inch-long treads stood half-buried in the earth. No trucks ever came or went along the access road, no one was ever there. I went and laid behind the enormous tombstones, staring at the clouds with the rifle across my chest. It was a quiet, thoughtless place, the way the world would be after a private catastrophe I longed for.

Several years later, in college, a friend of mine dragged me to a party in the basement of a fraternity house. There was no light, the only time you could see anything was when someone opened the door at the top of the stairs, and that lasted only for a second. I stumbled around. The whole room seemed to be made of corners. At one point, someone wedged open the door and I saw a few guys from the fraternity standing a few feet away. They were wearing night-vision goggles and smiling like ghouls.

My friend and I were only a little drunk. We went back to the dorm, listened to Meat Mortal records and drank from a bottle of 120 proof rum. After a while, he fell asleep and I went out to the common area. There was a girl sitting next to an open window. The wind kept lifting up the curtains, and she kept swatting them away. I didn't know her. I don't think she knew me. She had a lazy eye.

It was dark in her room. Sometimes a jitney or security van passed, splashing headlights onto the wall. I saw a plant next to the bed. Except for a few books, she kept her desk clean. I don't think we talked at all. We just sat down on the bed and she pinched out the buttons of her dress. Her skin was dusky and warm. But she had a cloying smell, like granulated honey.

I got up from the bed and hurried to the door. "What's wrong?" she asked. I fixed my jeans in the hallway. When I got back to the common area, I shuffled around. I went to look out the window. There were people I knew walking down the path, a theater couple holding hands and a gloomy art major resting a spear on his shoulder. Some of my friends had seen him skulking through the woods at night. He was the kind of person who said he was misunderstood and he was right, of course, but for the wrong reasons.

In the window's reflection, I saw her coming toward me, strangling the lapels of her robe. She wasn't crying. I'm not sure. I might've been. Again in her room, we didn't talk. I went to my knees and opened her robe. The bones of her pelvis felt like knife handles in my hands. I burrowed gently, chasing her breath. She seemed far away, her eyes closed, her head leaned to one side, and when the staircase shattered, she bent my neck back. We stayed like that a while, both of us breathing deeply.

Just as we were crossing 19th Street, several police officers rushed onto the avenue. They lifted their batons high into the air. A space opened between us and the thousands of protesters who'd already gone ahead. The police were cutting off the head of the snake. I watched a heavy woman on the new front line wave her arms and shout at the police officers. White spittle flew into the air. When she reached for something in her jacket, probably her phone, an officer slammed his baton down on her forearm, and the crowd exploded.

"Shame!"

"Shame!"

"Shame!"

The woman shoved the officer, but he maintained his balance enough to grab her and drag her into the empty space behind him. The others sealed the line. Infuriated, the protesters surged forward. Shouts came from every direction. Batons sliced through the crowd. A group of us splintered off, toppling the unguarded barricades. We scrambled across Irving and turned south onto Park as the bulk of the protesters followed. We swarmed over the cars. I saw a man in an SUV bury his face in his hands, and I wondered if he had an emergency or was simply annoyed. In the backseat of a taxi, a blonde woman in a crepe dress and dark sunglasses pretended to ignore us, while a guy in a Patagonia slapped a $20 bill against her driver's window. I couldn't tell if he was taunting the driver or trying to make up for the money the man was sure to lose. Maybe he was trying to buy the woman, maybe that's where we were now.

At Union Square, I climbed a traffic post for a better view. The sky was the icy blue of a credit card. I searched for you in the spellbound faces of the protesters. Everyone was rinsed in afternoon sunlight, exhilarated by freedom and violence, marching down the unplanned route, but none of them were you. The more people passed, the less they seemed to know about the altercation. They were just protesting, and their conversations drifted back to the inaccuracy of their job titles. Strange seductive explosions of laughter rang out. I rejoined the march, slipping in front of two boys in black leather trench coats. They were like twins with their thin mirrored sunglasses, although one was black and the other Asian.

"He starts out as a janitor," one said.

"Like Bruce Banner," the other replied.

"No, Banner is a scientist."

"Yeah, they're all losers who become vigilantes."

"Dr. Manhattan? He's beyond good and evil."

"What do you mean?"

"Like, a disease isn't good or bad, right?"

"No, diseases are bad."

"Toxic Avenger starts out a janitor and becomes King Kong, but he's been brought up in a moral universe. His aggression is—"

A man with dark sunglasses cut through the crowd, jostling me as he passed. I saw a flash of silver in his hand. Maybe a watch, maybe a knife. He seemed desperate to reach the sidewalk. When I regained my balance, I lost sight of him. Probably he escaped. The two boys continued their conversation behind me, as if they were completely alone, drinking bottomless cups of coffee at the all-night diner.

"With Harvey Keitel?"

"No, with Kim Bassinger and Russell Crowe."

"You're thinking of 'L.A. Confidential.'"

"It'd be better if it was called 'Bad Lieutenant.'"

"Well, it's not."

"There's the straight shooter, totally by the book. The second guy beats the shit out of everyone, he's beast mode. And the last one is just an asshole.

They have to team up to catch the bad guy. In the end, the asshole dies, one shot to the heart. The honest guy gets a promotion. But Russell Crowe wins, he's the beast, he bangs Kim Bassinger, who looks a lot like my mother, by the way, if Kim Bassinger had short dark hair and was Chinese."

As we approached Cooper Union, the crowd fell silent and slowed down. It took me several minutes to see what was going on. All the way down 7th Street, hundreds of naked men and women lay on the ground. They were arranged in a pattern, like a chain or a helix, that ran to Second Avenue. Almost all the nudes were white, several very pale, though there were black and brown bodies too, just very few of them, and they were all piled on each other like fallen dominoes, their faces to the sky and their arms and legs pressed against their sides. A large white man with several lanyards around his neck shot the nudes with a heavy-looking camera.

It was odd how uniform they were. They were completely exposed, they'd revealed themselves to the world, their true selves, and yet they all looked more or less the same. Still, close to me, I saw a woman speckled with so many moles that she looked like outer space, and a man with a scar down the center of his chest. And then I thought of things I couldn't see. What were the people thinking about? What did their voices sound like, or their laughs, their heartbeats? How many had ever fallen in love? How many were in love right now, and were you one of them? Was I? I scanned the bodies on the ground but I didn't know how to pick you out. You could've been anyone.

I leapt over the barricade, scraping against the canvas jacket of the bearded man beside me, which angered him, and he pushed me down as I landed. My fall drew the attention of the photographer, who pointed at me and yelled. I could see the darkness inside his mouth. Some of the nudes pivoted to see who he was yelling at. I got to my feet just as the man with the beard came over the fence.

He swung at me, but I jumped back. His fist glanced off my shoulder. Behind him, drawn to chaos, a few protesters hopped over the barricade. One of them had tied over his mouth a strip of black cloth printed with a skull's jawbones and teeth. They raced past me as the man with the beard lunged again. This time, he buried his shoulder into my ribs, and we crashed onto the ground. The back of my head smacked the pavement. I closed my eyes. I heard him snarl but the sound was flattened by a chorus of boots, horses' hooves, screams, metal crashing against the street, helicopter blades.

I twisted free and scrambled to my feet. The nudes ran. Several protesters were giving chase and the police knifed after them. I hurried down the street in hopes that I could still find you, that I could still protect you. But on the next avenue, chain-linked cages lined the sidewalk, and the police shoved the runaways and protesters inside.

Above us, a flare flashed and exploded into smoke. Another shattered the upper display windows of a commercial building. Glass fell in a violent cascade. I raced from cage to cage, searching the prisoners' faces. At the fourth, I found you at last. I looked into your eyes. They were so gray and afraid, but no, they weren't your eyes, your eyes were different, and your face looked older now, as if all its leaves had fallen. You clawed at the links. There was blood on your arm but I couldn't tell if it was yours.

Behind me there was a row of abandoned information booths for different political action groups—I saw signs for Lyndon LaRouche and Block the Bombs—and I snatched a heavy paperweight from a stack of pamphlets and smashed open the door. A tall German man with bleached white hair rushed out. In his haste he knocked me down. The other prisoners bounded from the cage and scattered, disappearing into the crevices between buildings. I thought I'd lost you again but when I got to my feet, I saw you standing before a rider. He was blocking out the sun with his upper body, and his horse had lifted its front hooves into the air. The policeman raised his baton to strike you but I leapt in front. I punched the horse in the throat. I hit it as hard as I could. I knocked it off balance. It fell onto its side, trapping the policeman underneath. He didn't say anything. He just stared at me as if I were his own loathsome son.

I held out my hand to you. But someone I didn't see pulled you away. Young boys in rags surrounded me. All of them held armfuls of stones. The first struck me below the eye. The one who threw it was no more than nine, heroically simpering. The others jeered. I covered my skull as the stones rained down. It felt like I was falling through hatchets. My skin split apart like rotten fruit. I looked up. I shouldn't have, but I was desperate to see where they'd taken you. A stone broke my jaw. I could taste the copper blood. Whether it was exhaustion or a submission to the inevitable, I unwrapped my arms from my skull and everything went dark.

Time passed. I don't know how long. I heard the hum of an outdoor machine, maybe a generator, and a jackhammer slapping up the concrete. Cars swished along the avenue, overpowered by the sound of an exhausted bus, and from across the street, bits of conversation floated over. The voices had the suffocating quality of a heavy afternoon sleep. I strained to hear the words but learned nothing.

I had no idea what time it was. I couldn't see the light because my eyes were either encrusted with blood or I was blind. I guessed that it was morning. The air was cold, as if the sun hadn't had a chance. When I tried to roll onto my side, the pain refused me, and I gasped and fell back onto my stomach.

When I woke the second time, I had only enough strength to lift myself up before collapsing again. I saw nothing but the sounds were different. I heard water sloshing around, and then felt a wet cloth tamp against my wounds. I smelled a familiar smell of rot on someone's breath, as if a piece of food had become stuck inside their gums and had turned rancid over the course of many days. The stranger washed me many times, slopping a cloth through the water and dragging it across my skin. I didn't think of you, that it could be you. I didn't think of anything.

When I woke again, I was alone, and managed to peel myself from the ground for the refuge of a wooden bench. I could see now. There were trees. I was in a park. It was almost evening. I must've been dragged, or crawled. It didn't matter. People drifted by, two Korean girls in matching denim jackets, a young boy dragging a greasy shih tzu, a white punk with highlighter yellow hair.

I wondered how much time had passed, and whether the war had begun, and if I'd be able to tell from the strangers' behavior. Probably not, I guessed. Fear in their eyes, sorrow in their hearts, reckless laughter signifying nothing. It would all look the same. War would be our last resort, the president had assured us. But war was our natural state. War was our economy. He knew we craved aggression, that we longed to praise our virtuous boys slaughtered in cities of dust. He knew in time he'd be remembered as all presidents are remembered, as a complicated man.

A man in shabby green coveralls walked by with a long mechanical claw, picking up trash. A few pigeons fluttered into the air and then landed again once he passed. I scanned the rest of the park, looking for some sign of what had happened, and I wondered where you were. I didn't know if it was you in the cage. I didn't know if you were you, or if you were something else, something outside of you. I stood up from the bench to inspect myself, my torn clothes and the gashes and bruises all over my body, and then I limped out of the park and went back into the city, to find you.

The Father

When Angie called he was washing the bottoms of his shoes, concerned that his soles were soiled with the runoff of other donors. Angie had tried to call his wife but couldn't get through, she said. She quickly confessed that she and her husband were getting a divorce. The man wiped his tongue on his sleeve. He had a cat hair in his mouth. Angie asked if he was there. "Yes," he said. "Can you meet me?" she asked. He had an appointment at the sperm bank later that afternoon. He wondered aloud if she'd drive to the parking lot of the strip mall, the one with the small movie theater.

"Near the outer banks," she confirmed.

Yes. Okay. Three p.m. Three p.m. They hung up.

He ran his hands under the tap water and washed them with Palmolive. He then removed the cat hair. Upon further examination he discovered it wasn't a cat hair. It looked more like a sweater thread or the fiber from a carpet. He didn't have a cat.

Months before, he and Angie had chanced a bottle of wine while Sarah was away. Angie had twirled her hair nervously with her forefinger, curling it over and over. She tinkered with the salt and pepper shakers, sliding them around like chess queens while she and Abe made small talk. When he asked if she was feeling okay, she admitted to a spate of recent panic attacks. She said she was afraid of her own pubic hair, scared to talk to men on the telephone. She'd come to believe her own menstrual blood was some kind of corruption. She looked into the mirror and saw a monster. The man listened sympathetically. He looked her in the eye affirmingly but kept glancing at her mouth. It was like the zipper of a purse with lots of money inside. She said that a long time ago she'd been afraid of losing her teeth, and remembered a childhood bike accident in which she skidded on sand and flew over the handlebars, smashing her mouth onto the curb. Her lip ripped into a chunk.

At the hospital the doctor discovered two of her teeth missing and suggested she may have swallowed them. The man noticed the slightest furrow in her lip where the doctor had sewn stitches. Her makeup helped disguise the scar, but he could still see it. Angie drank her wine, resting the glass on her lower lip. Her eyes closed. Her teeth clicked against the glass. He imagined her eating a salad, the sound of the fork sliding from her mouth, the scrape of metal against her teeth.

"I don't see anything," he said.

"I know you can," she paused. "It was when Sandy turned six that I became afraid of losing my teeth. I know those kinds of dreams mean you feel powerless, but then I remembered the bike accident, which happened when I was six."

He reached for Angie's shoulder and squinched it in his hand.

"Now Sandy's got her period," she said. "I think all these anxieties are related. I think I'm reexperiencing puberty because she just turned thirteen."

The man did not have kids, but he'd heard of parents who rediscovered themselves when they had children. It always sounded like a wonderful experience. They found their optimistic purpose, they could see a million shades of green again. They were happy. But Angie sounded harried, like she'd split into two different people, one rooted in the present, the other drowning in the ocean of the past. He wanted to console her but he didn't know what to say. It sounded so dramatic. He placed his hand on hers and raised his eyebrows suggestively as he tilted the bottle toward her, offering her more wine. She made fists inside her sweater.

"Just a little," she said.

Shortly after she left, he finished the wine. It had been a gift, an extra bottle from a party, he couldn't remember, something Sarah wouldn't miss. He sat down at the table, thinking of Angie and wondering about his own parents, if they'd ever experienced similar anxieties. Counting back, his mother had been thirty-four and his father thirty-seven when he was born. In ten months he would be thirty-seven. His wife had never wanted children, but lately he'd become surprisingly enthusiastic. In his mind he saw a strange reflection of himself, a gruff figure holding in his arms a tiny piglet whose skin was downy pink. Delicate white lashes made abbreviated canopies over its eyes, and a soft flank draped over his bearish forearm. Though it was a slight inverse of what Angie had been talking about, his recent desire to have children and the discovered age of his father seemed like an odd coincidence, emanations of the same invisible government. He was half his father's body, and he speculated there could be a time release in his DNA, contingent on the moment he transitioned from one parent into the other. Maybe there was a code inside him, an envelope mailed many years ago that had finally opened.

When the wine was finished he poured himself a whiskey. The late afternoon moved into the hollow blue of twilight as he stirred at the kitchen table, ruminating over the possibility of children. People called it a miracle. It seemed more like a pleasant math. When Sarah came home he got up from his chair abruptly, gripped her by the arms and pushed her against the stove. "I'm thinking about kids," he said.

He found Angie's SUV in the parking lot and pulled up beside her the way police officers do. Angie looked as if she'd been sleeping in the woods. Her hair was knotted and her eyes frenzied with makeup. He nodded and got out of his car. The interior of her SUV was disheveled, too, the floor flooded with maps, newspapers, Kleenex and plastic rings from six-packs. Angie had a beer in her hand and reached into the backseat for another. She smelled vaguely of chicken soup. Ash and white butts battled inside the ashtray. Marlboro Lights were the one cigarette he could resist. The uniquely acrid smoke repulsed him, or maybe it was the whiteness. With other cigarettes he smelled toast and firewood. With Marlboro Lights it was just chemicals. Angie lit one and resumed her anxious confession. She and Bob were getting a divorce. He'd told her they were intellectually incompatible. He was seeing another woman, a librarian he'd met on the Internet. Angie had threatened to give him a vasectomy with a kitchen knife. "Now I have to find a condo, something cheap for me and Sandy, and I have to get a better job, maybe doing data entry." He rubbed his hand comfortingly across her thigh, smoothing errant bits of ash into her blue jeans. She mewed softly into her beer. He tried to console her, telling her it was not her fault. He never liked Bob. Barbeque Bob. No more big government Bob. But did he not like Bob because Bob was Bob?

He couldn't help but see the opportunity. Angie would almost certainly share his infidelity, he was confident, but it was an ugly thought and he tried to shake it by looking out the window. He listened to her detail Bob's vulgarities, the disgust he provoked in her. Bob never talked to Sandy anymore. Bob never flossed and his breath smelled like bread products. The man floated between her words, her voice scratchy from crying and smoking. He turned back toward her. She had a good body, a little loose in the cage but nice. She reached for his hand. He felt himself uncoiling. He turned to the window, again trying to break the sudden swoon, and he saw the sperm bank out the window, the site of so much self-pleasure and guiltless benefaction. Angie stroked his wrist. A man opened the tinted door of the sperm bank and strode to his car, a dark blazer draped over his shoulder. He wore sunglasses. The man turned to Angie, reached around her shoulder and brought her closer. She looked frightened, a deer in the field that hears thunder, and he closed his eyes, found her mouth, and kissed her. The musty unwashed smell of her hair rushed into his nostrils. Her lips were tight but he could feel her tongue flicker. She suddenly relaxed. She surrendered quickly. He could have sex with her if he wanted. She was thirty-five. He would leave Sarah, or Sarah would leave him, it didn't matter who left whom. He would have sex with Angie and then a child would come, a dream that Sarah didn't share, and he would inherit Sandy, too, Angie's daughter. He'd have two children. Love was specious. Sandy would become his daughter. His erection swelled. He imagined Angie and nubile Sandy, lying naked on a king-sized bed, side by side, their legs crooked in the air, both of them wet and open, supine and waiting for him to enter, mother and daughter holding hands, their eyes the same color, both of them ready.

Privately he had been charting Sarah's period. He wrote down the days of the week in a blue notebook, marking with an "X" the days Sarah menstruated, and "O" on the days she did not. He read about ovulation and the mysterious LH surge at the library, and discovered there was a coveted window between the eleventh and twentieth day of a woman's cycle, when the luteinizing hormone peaked and her fertility was maximized. The reference book discouraged couples from having sex every day. "Decrease in sperm motility acutely lowers the probability of achieving pregnancy. Increase in frequency of sex hampers the likelihood of fertilization," it said. On a lark, the man went over to the library computer and fished around for pharmaceutical websites. He'd ordered Ambien before. Maybe they had fake birth control. Within a few clicks he found the familiar hexagonal packaging in a small photograph. It was the same pink cartridge Sarah used, but the pills were counterfeit. They were made of sugar. "For *happy accidents*," the copy read. "Sometimes babies just *slip through the cracks*." He was disappointed that a whole market had been designed for people like him, men and women conniving against their partners. He'd thought his sudden scheme unique.

He and Sarah made love infrequently. When they did have sex, they performed dispassionately, their bodies efficient like machines. He'd come to want her only for production, and she used sex to disappear. They'd lost their common purpose. The man became lazy in his enticements, dragging his erection across her thigh while she read from her Coetzee novel in bed. He used alcohol as his only aphrodisiac. He offered to stimulate her with Altoids but she told him that was gross. His friend Wanda had mentioned it, and told him how her boyfriend seduced her. While they watched an NBA game on TV he'd scoop her off the couch and throw her onto the bed. Then he'd pull it out and slap her across the cheeks until he was fully hard. She'd scream and giggle, is what she said. He didn't know why she told him. Maybe it wasn't any stranger than a porcupine urinating on his mate, or a lake duck using his penis as a lasso, but it seemed brutish. Sarah often put down her novel and slipped off her pajama bottoms wordlessly. What did it matter. In a million years what would anything matter, he thought, whether she wanted a child. They would be gone, all of humanity would be gone. The universe was contracting. Soon there wouldn't be any stars to look at, to make patterns out of. Stars like a hundred million sperm scattered across the night sky.

Sarah didn't want to make the sacrifice. She liked things as they were.

She didn't want a kid to vomit all over her cashmere sweater and leave crumbs in between the car seats. Kids were expensive. Her breasts would become spigots. The exterior controls, the murky cave, doctors and money, no wine, no sushi. She'd be forced to drink fish oil. It was the final frontier, the patriarch exacting control over the woman's body, mandating her behavior, lording over her controls. He listened to her grievances and tried to persuade her. "It's not a sacrifice I want to make," she said. "And why do you want children now, out of the blue? They're always sick." He said once the baby came, their shared futility would disappear. She told him she didn't "share futility." He was surprised she didn't want a child, even though they agreed early in their relationship not to have children. Women were supposed to have clocks. Instead, an alarm had gone off inside of him. The species was commanding his scrotal brain. He no longer cared who set the alarm.

Lobbying her was not going to help, he realized. Sarah would have to be pregnant to want a child. Over time the science would bear out. He just had to be patient. While he'd never know the exact day of her LH surge, if they had sex every other day between the eleventh and twentieth day of her cycle, the odds were fifty-fifty. Just a coin flip. He didn't want pressure. He'd heard of couples who wanted kids too much, who were unable to achieve pregnancy because they fixated too hard. He took Xanax. He stopped at the local Qi Gong massage parlor, allowing himself to be handled by a brusque woman with shoveler's hands. He smoked joints in the backyard. If Sarah got pregnant he'd have to dissuade her from having an abortion. He might not even know she was pregnant. She might not tell him, though she did discuss her menstruation with him, how her flow had gotten heavier. He eavesdropped when she telephoned her gynecologist. "I'm way off schedule and it's just gushing," she informed the doctor. In replacing her birth control with sugar pills he'd tapped into a violent flood. He didn't know if that meant she was more or less fertile. Some women were just dead birds inside.

He was a primitive. A sewer. But Angie had talked about her unconscious connection with Sandy. It was her fault he linked the two. He felt the undertow of his desire pulling him down, his fingertips pulsing with caress as he slipped his hand under the fold of her blouse, spreading his fingers like a starfish over the round polyester cup of her bra. They closed their eyes together. "Open your mouth," he said, and they kissed like teenagers in a dark van, their world small and meaningful. He was feeling her breast, the precocious eighth-grade breast of a girl he fooled around with in middle school who'd probably just gotten her period. He remembered Jessica, the first girl he'd seen shirtless. She'd shrugged off her oversized V-neck. She told him he could do anything he wanted and he'd frozen with opportunity. Her ribs, her collarbones exposed. A mole on her abdomen. She gave him too much power in her permission. He felt unprepared.

"Where are you going?" she asked, lighting a cigarette.

He hadn't thought of her in years until he was poking around the Internet one night, spying on old acquaintances. He found Krystyn living in California with a blank-faced computer programmer and two Dobermans. The website said she liked dogs and chocolate. He saw photographs of their house, tear sheets of Ikea furniture. Heather was an associate director at a marketing company in Boston. She'd always been a part of the solution. He typed Jessica's name into the computer. She'd moved away in ninth grade. It was his long regret he walked away from her, afraid. The only link was to an obituary. Jessica had died of heart failure. She was only thirty-two. He stared at the screen, the pixilated photograph and scanned text. When they'd kissed he was peach fuzz. She smoked moodily and ate ranch Doritos, covering up the smell of both with Certs. In the photograph she was fat and smiled like a balloon. Three oversized children surrounded her. She didn't look remotely the same, but she looked happy.

Sandy looked like Angie. He thought of the daughter as he began to unbutton her blouse, kissing her on the neck, smelling the perfume and smoke from her cigarettes. What would have happened to Jessica if he'd stayed? Would she have died? Angie's hands wrapped around his head. She was locking her fingers into his hair. Lightly pulling tufts. He grabbed her hand and pushed it against his jeans. He wanted to show her he'd changed. She unlatched her seat belt from the cartridge and moved onto him, reaching for the lever to lower his seatback into a horizontal position. He felt the conflict of raw desire and futility. What do you shout. He massaged her shoulders, a distancing move, trying to buy time. Should he do it. She was Sarah's friend. She was so yielding. He bit her lower lip. She pulled away, touching her mouth to see if it was bleeding. She stared at him with a suspicious slant.

He couldn't count on Angie. She was the lottery. She might get pregnant but probably wouldn't and if she did she'd abort it without telling him. There'd be no way to prevent it without being overt. Afterward she'd be ashamed of what they did and she'd feel repulsed by him. She'd think he took advantage of her when she was at her lowest point. The betrayal would be unforgivable. Angie moved back toward him and they began again. She reached against his thigh and he bit her lip again, an invitation instead of protest. Her eyes widened with enthusiasm. He covered himself in swathes of her hair so that she couldn't see his face. Her unbuttoned shirt draped over him like two sides of a tent.

The sperm bank had offered fewer complications. It wasn't parenting; it was rudimentary reproduction. He'd been going there for weeks, after a pregnancy never obtained with Sarah. He hadn't enjoyed the deception anyway. Perhaps the deceit prevented pregnancy. Sarah seemed much happier once her cycle regulated, after he abandoned the sugar pills. She felt like herself again. When she remarked that the color and shape of her pills had returned to old, he said, "They probably were giving you a generic." He'd already moved on to plan B. He'd reproduce himself in strangers. Weeks ago he'd made an appointment and drove there on a weekday afternoon. The sperm bank lurked anonymously between a dry cleaner's and a Russian chess shop at the adobe-colored strip mall. He loitered anxiously outside, admiring a set of handsome pawns. He felt nervous. At the desk a young man in a pink polo recorded his name and handed him a clipboard with fill-in-the-blank forms. The room was painted dead salmon. Innocuous unframed prints of watercolor flowers papered the walls. He stared at the prints until a white woman with lavender scrubs called his name. She was not attractive. Her eyes sagged. He followed her through a long hallway. He'd come psychologically prepared to masturbate. There were doors to his left and right, and he imagined stobby men with their pants around their ankles tugging on their joints, every one of them ejaculating into a clear plastic receptacle. He was nervous about the cup. Would it spill. Would he fail to fill it.

They sat down on steel chairs in a bright examination room. The woman asked why he wanted to be a donor. The man explained his situation with Sarah. He wanted to contribute something meaningful to the world but he was only one man. He felt compelled, like it wasn't really his decision. It was more or less the truth. The woman asked if he knew that some of the clients who sought out fertility centers were single mothers, lesbians, and surrogates for gay men. He shrugged his shoulders.

"You'll take tests to determine your eligibility, and we'll document your income, education history, medical history, hobbies, religious preferences, vices, anything pertinent to evaluate your suitability. You'll need to provide photographs from different periods of your life. People will want to know what they're getting. What does your wife think about this?"

"I haven't told her."

"That's not a good sign. Also, I'm sorry to be candid, but you're a little old to be a donor."

"I'm thirty-six."

The intake nurse scribbled onto a sheet of paper.

"Are you saying I can't be a donor?"

"We'll see," she said.

The rest of the screening consisted of data surveys, blood and DNA tests, and a cardiac and respiratory discovery. Everything was in line. The man was cleared to donate sperm, but his file would be coded with an orange stripe, meaning his sperm was "mature." Orange stripes were deterrents. Most parents-to-be wanted virile, twentysomething Harvard grads. The next week he dropped off a large portfolio of his photocopied transcripts, college degrees (not Harvard), tax statements, bank statements, broad brushstrokes of his medical and dental histories, proof of employment, and his birth certificate. He provided photographs of his infancy, childhood, adolescence, and a few from his twenties and early thirties, so potential parents could preview half the possibility of their future child. He included one his mother took of him at twelve years old, straddling his bicycle in the driveway with a bag of newspapers slung over his shoulder. He knew it would be appealing. In the photograph he looked dignified. Patrolling the streets early in the morning when the lawns were glazed with frost and everyone slept warmly in their beds, it was as if he were the only one alive, and it gave him a special pride. But in its sixth month the pastoral paper route was interrupted by a bellicose German Shepherd, which sprang from a set of hedges and toppled him off his bike, begging its sharp teeth into his upper thigh. The boy howled in pain. He tried to wriggle free but the dog clamped down harder and shook its head violently back and forth, trying to pull off a chunk. Suddenly the boy woke up, surrounded by adults. One of the men had a shotgun with its barrel to the blacktop. He strained to see the German Shepherd and found it lying parallel on the nearby grass. A woman handed him some paper towels. A week after the scabs healed he started to develop the scar. The dog's mouth was imprinted on him, and would always be there, a tiny iridescent constellation of tooth marks.

He visited the sperm bank twice a week, on Tuesdays and Fridays. They requested he not ejaculate for at least forty-eight hours prior to appointments. Sex with Sarah suffered as a result, but neither seemed to mind. Soon the man developed a routine. The receptionist handed him a plastic container and directed him to the available room. Locked inside, he carefully removed his clothes, stepping on the tops of his shoes to avoid direct contact with the carpet, and he hung each item from a peg on the far wall. He placed them in the order of how he'd get dressed: sweater, jeans, shirt, underwear. He then replaced his shoes, standing otherwise naked in the room. Ignoring the tattered magazines, he played the same DVD on the all-in-one TV and skipped to a scene with a voluptuous blonde woman on her knees fellating a hairy man in a Mexican wrestling mask. The woman's painted fingernails raked the wrestler's vulgar abdomen, and he tousled her hair and murmured as she moved on him with a delicate rhythm until the wrestler raptured simultaneously with him, the actor onto the blonde woman's chin and chest and he against the lip of the clear plastic receptacle.

That November he had gone to see his father. On the way he dropped by his old hometown, East New Chesterwick, a blip of fast-food restaurants and tangents of woods in southern Ohio. He threaded the streets until he came to his old neighborhood and parked his car at the turnoff. The streets were wet from a recent shower. Squiggled worms had emerged and many anthills pocked the edges. As a boy he'd fingered sand into their holes, spreading out the mounds, but the ants emerged resiliently from the cracks. Their broad empire was never in danger. The sky was overcast, gray like faded clothes. The homes were evenly spaced apart as buttons on a shirt, and on his right thick pines made dark lines that grew into pallid shadows. He'd loved those woods when he was younger. He'd played war with his friends, splitting into teams and using sturdy Y-shaped sticks for guns. They smeared mud onto their faces and stayed out past sunset, arguing over who shot whom and where to store the munitions. When he was in high school, he walked through the woods alone, beheading ferns and skunkweed plants, filling the air with their foul defense. There was a faraway area he liked to visit, a campsite or a pagan place, he didn't know, a semicircle of stones surrounded by mossy trunks and half logs. It'd been abandoned. Occasionally he removed his clothes and sat naked in the middle of the circle, listening to the quiet and feeling the cool air against his skin. Sometimes he made himself hard and rubbed it against the earth, as if trying to cross something out. The site was on an incline, and he stood on the edge and surveyed the expanse, pinecones and trees and poison ivy and downed branches replicating themselves far into the distance like a video game. He listened to the birds warn others of his presence.

His sister told him to be prepared. She said their old house would look very Japanese. He hadn't seen it for twenty years. In their photographs it remained the same, a red ranch with evergreen bushes towering over a mum garden, and a blue Nova parked in the driveway. He could see the house in the distance, grayish brown instead of red, but he paused as something grabbed his eye. It was an animal carcass, a rabbit's body crumpled on the short grass. When he got close enough he saw that its head was missing. On one end a bushy white-dot tail tipped into the air, and little legs built for bounding were now folded in sleep. At the front there wasn't any blood. The neckline wasn't raw. But the rabbit had been decapitated. The cut was neat and straight. He guessed a person had killed the rabbit and used an electric saw or a similar tool. He crouched and stroked the rabbit's coarse dead fur. Fleas still swarmed through its hair. Flies buzzed near its tail.

He walked more slowly now toward his old house. He passed Frank Volvano's driveway and surmised they no longer lived there. The Volvanos were not mini-van people. Many years ago he and Frank planned to go as soldiers on Halloween. In preparation he'd painted cadmium green and yellow patches onto a pair of blue jeans and sweatshirt to simulate camouflage. But his costume was the opposite of camouflage. He stuck out like a fire. The colors were intensely bright, and after the paint dried, his jeans and sweatshirt became coarse and stiff all over. The paint scratched his skin when he walked. That summer he'd discovered a helmet in his basement and planned to wear it. It was stony and grey and had a white eagle painted on the side. The helmet was heavy when he tried it on, like having two heads. He asked his father where it came from. It was his grandfather's from the war. He thought that meant his grandfather had worn it into combat, but later he saw in an encyclopedia of World War II that the helmet was German, and he realized his grandfather had retrieved it off a dead man, maybe even one he'd killed. On Halloween he ate dinner at the Volvano's house and was served chicken and Spanish rice, which inspired Frank's brother Bon to spew vitriolically about Puerto Ricans. He claimed that Puerto Ricans wore pointed-toe shoes because they were always climbing chain-link fences to escape from prison. Then they'd go dancing. When Frank put on his outfit, he looked like steel, dressed head to toe in camouflage with face paint and a pair of black combat boots. He carried a fake M-16 and there were two plastic hand grenades clasped to his belt loops. In contrast, Abe looked like a mistake. He was like the scarecrow version of a soldier, a three-year old's drawing of an army man. The only thing that gave him authenticity was his grandfather's Nazi helmet. "Go get yourself some Ricans," Bon said, punching Frank in the arm.

Six more houses and he came to his own. It was as his sister described. The red paint had been stripped away and replaced with taupe, and in the front yard bonsai topiary surrounded a petite rock garden. The new tenants had excavated the evergreen bushes and planted hulking stalks of thick bamboo. The house seemed much smaller than he remembered, but it was a completely different place. Whoever lived there was different. He could see a woman through the main window, white, with an ivory sweater, older by twenty years. She was looking into another room, dipping into a mug. He'd intended to ring the doorbell but changed his mind. The woman seemed so cozy. He stood there for five full minutes, just staring at the house, hoping she would notice him and ask him inside for cider. He would decline, and give her a strong, stoical look.

"Can I help you?" a voice boomed.

He was startled. He turned to face an obese neighbor, who wore a winter coat over his pajamas and was holding a silver thermos.

"This used to be my house," he said defensively, pointing toward the Japanese home.

The neighbor scrutinized him. "Silva, is it? Abe Silva? Oh yes, about thirty years ago. In fact, you used to play with my daughter Anna."

The man pretended to have trouble remembering.

"Anna is a lawyer now."

"I'm a lawyer, too," he lied. "Did Anna used to call you by your first name? Stan? And your wife is Gail?"

"She still does that. It drives us crazy." The neighbor paused. "You sang 'Bette Davis Eyes' in our living room. Into a carrot."

"I don't remember that."

He smiled nostalgically. "The last time I saw you, you asked Anna to be part of your private club, you and Frank," he said, pointing to the house in the distance. Abe flushed slightly at the memory. "I don't know if you heard what happened to Bon Volvano?" the neighbor asked.

"No."

"A few years ago he hiked up the highway ravine and shot himself in the head."

"Bon killed himself?"

"Yes, with a shotgun. He put it in his mouth."

It seemed an awful detail to share. He paused. "What kind of law does

Anna do?"

"Boat law," her father answered. "You were going to initiate her, remember? You had a stick that was cut and bent in the middle. You were on my front steps and threatened to pinch her arm with the stick. You didn't see me standing behind the screen door and I scared the shit out of you. Scared shitless. You ran all the way home."

"I hid in the basement."

"And then you moved that year?"

He looked back at his old house, then turned toward the neighbor. "Bon killed himself?"

A few hours later he stood in front of his father's house, looking for movement inside the window. He'd already rang the doorbell six times. Weeks ago they'd made a plan to move a credenza into storage, then watch the Ohio State-Indiana game. Probably they'd order the pizza with fried vegetables from Little Tony's. Because his father's car was in the driveway, he began to worry. It was possible his father had suffered a head injury and was bleeding on the floor inside. He could be dead in the bathtub. Or in bed, having passed away in the night. A heart attack. He imagined his father sleeping, or appearing to sleep, the long hump of his body covered with a yellow wool blanket, the one they made him use when he'd been ill. It was the extra blanket. His father never threw anything away. He probably had the same long johns from forty years ago. The man called his father's landline and could hear the phone ringing inside. His cell phone had gone straight to voice mail. Consistently his father had denied him a key to the house, and similarly, he'd refused to hide a spare, the way other families did, like under the ceramic chipmunk named "Nuts" that guarded the entranceway. His father had acquired custody of Nuts after the divorce. It was a spiteful request as part of the settlement – his mother had once thrown Nuts at his father's head. His father claimed it would ward off other evil spirits. He considered it a talisman, a mark of his survival, and bitterly he'd placed it on the lawn.

The man felt a nagging sense of urgency. When he'd imagined his father injured on the floor, it had been a fleeting thought, but the longer he idled there, the more he believed in the possibility. How else to explain the car in the driveway? He considered his options. Calling the police, breaking in, waiting, leaving, checking with neighbors, or yelling out his father's name. He did not think positively, and did not believe himself an inviolable force the way many men do, and so he resigned himself to a paradox: If he broke into the house, his father would be fine, and would have a very rational, unexplored reason for having locked the front door, left the car in the driveway, and not answered his phone. As a result, the man would be embarrassed. But if he didn't break into the house, or if he waited for the police or a neighbor, his father would die, and he'd have lost the opportunity to save him in these critical moments. He would feel guilty for the rest of his life. It was like the probability equation about God, that it was better to believe he exists, because the reward for having faith was so much better than the punishment for not. The man did not believe in God, but he decided the obvious thing to do was break in, ensuring the safety of his father. He hurried to the front door and hurled Nuts through the window. Glass shattered in and outside the house. A shard raked the back of his hand. He pulled the cut to his mouth and sipped, grabbing jagged pieces off the frame with his other hand and flicking them onto the lawn. Removing his jacket, he laid it across the window and hoisted himself up, ready to enter. Suddenly he was yanked back by his belt loops. He was pulled from the house before he'd even managed to get his head inside. The man turned around. It was his father.

"What the hell are you doing?"

"I thought you might be—"

"This is my house."

"You didn't answer the phone."

"Fuck the phone. This is my house."

When the universe became vapor and all of space was diminished, whether this individual got enough sleep or why that person committed murder would no longer be relevant. It never was. Yet the man felt burdened with his private obligation. Everything was a metaphor, a transparent imitation of life. Only his purpose, his desire to have children—ordered by nature, his ancestors, caprice, or whatever – mattered. When that mission was accomplished, he could rest.

He pushed Angie away and stared at her with cold neutrality. She moved off him and rolled down her window, letting in a rash of sunlight. She looked like a violent afternoon.

"I can't do this," he said.

"Why? Because of Sarah," she muttered.

"Not because of Sarah," he answered begrudgingly. "Because I don't think you'd go through with it."

She smiled demurely and grabbed his hand to demonstrate her permission, to show him she'd have sex with him. She was vulnerable like a teenager, feeling the sand of her desire passing through a stranger's fingers. "Please," she said.

"No," he said curtly, pulling it back. "The only reason I want to have sex with you is to get you pregnant."

Angie paused before answering, allowing time for the sounds of the words to fulfill their meaning. "For fuck's sake."

"I want a fucking baby. I want to fuck you and make a baby."

"Fuck you."

"I'm like a single fucking arrow." He paused. "You and Sandy should stay at our place."

She threw her half can of beer at his face, partly because she was so angry and partly because it would snap her back into reality. It bounced off his shoulder and splat against the window. Everything he said was absurd. "Why should I stay there?"

"Because I'm not coming back," he said.

He was late by fifteen minutes. "Door six," the receptionist winked, handing him a plastic container. When he entered the room he tried to let go. The sperm bank was a kind of sanctuary for him, a place of pure male purpose. He washed his hands in the small basin opposite the wall of magazines. He was no longer hard from the car. There was a full-size mirror near the television – apparently some guys liked to watch themselves, or maybe it was just for grooming – and he smoothed the hair above his ears, the way men did in movies, by spitting on his hands, rubbing them together, and flattening the sides. Occasionally when he masturbated he spit on his hand, but he tried to resist that urge because as a lubricant spit was short-lived and afterward his hand smelled like something worse than drool. He kept looking in the mirror. He felt guilty about Angie. He'd been rude. He had started to use her, had wanted to, he'd almost gone through with it. He felt like a thousand puzzle pieces. Sarah would know. Angie would tell her. But he'd already left her long ago, in trying to get her pregnant. He'd been in disarray, scattered like the stars, arranged imperfectly and with violence like the constellation on his thigh.

He left the room and returned to the receptionist, asking for additional containers.

"What happened to the one I gave you?" the receptionist asked.

"I just want to have a lot of them," the man insisted.

"You can only make one deposit every three days. Otherwise the count will not be high enough."

"Just give them to me, prick," he said tersely.

He loomed over the desk. It was an awkward request, but the receptionist shoved a half dozen more onto the counter. The man ferried them back to room six, where he placed them in a row on top of the television set. There was no lock on the door, so he dragged a metal chair and clipped it under the doorknob, barricading himself in. He pushed the television console against the door, too, and the fire extinguisher, the DVD shelf, the magazine shelf, and a space heater. It wouldn't last forever. In fact the receptionist had probably reported him to the security for behaving strangely. Whatever. He removed all his clothes like usual, stepping on his shoes, preventing his feet from touching the carpet. And then he kicked his shoes away. And took off his socks. He no longer cared about the runoff. He began to stroke himself, and it jumped up quickly, enthusiastic after such recent discard. He masturbated, bringing himself to climax right away, ejaculating into one cup, waiting, repeating, and then into another. He imagined nothing. There were no images, just the room. He stared only at the cups, filling each of them to the best of his ability. On the last one, as gruff men shouted outside and bashed their shoulders against the door to his room, he thought of the man his grandfather killed, the soldier lying stiff on the sidewalk with a bullet in his heart, a city of cement around him. He could almost see the German's face.

The actress got there first.

"Did you know people used to eat raccoons for Thanksgiving?" she asked. "A restaurant in Echo Park is serving it now. It's very retro."

"Have you tried it?" I asked.

"No, but I hear all sorts of things about food. Lobster was trash, then they served it on trains. Did you know that? I find eating so tedious. I wish it came in a pill."

"I like food," I said.

"We'll be dining on cockroaches soon. It's only a matter of time."

"Where did you hear that?"

"When I was a young girl, I showed promise and was sent to a theater for the gifted and talented, and one of the things the director had us do was to rub our legs together like crickets. We were all lying on our backs with shorts on and our legs wriggling in the air. What a dirty old man."

She sighed and pushed a choppy black wig toward the cashier.

"What are you going as?" I asked.

She looked up suddenly, as if a bird had flown into the bank.

"Do you hear that?" she asked.

"What?"

"The sound."

"No. I don't hear anything."

"That's good. That's very good. You're very lucky," she said, turning to me. "It's for a friend."

"Twenty-eight, no tax," the cashier said.

The bodyguard pressed against the counter and slid a hundred-dollar bill onto the glass.

"I can't change that," the cashier said.

"Do what you got to do, bro," he said.

People always say the difference between the East Coast and the West Coast is how people behave in line. To me, it's the hills. The ones in California make me calm in the way only certain landscapes can—they're smooth and round, with the appearance of elephant skin, as if we were living on the surface of a large animal—and they have a vastly different effect on me than the heavily wooded hills of the northeast, which brood like old wizards. I could see why my father left. I mean, as far as landscapes go, though I don't suppose that had anything to do with it. Though what did anything have to do with anything—I didn't come for the hills either.

I found him in the common room seated in a wheelchair, wearing a black hooded robe and holding a plastic scythe. Paper skeletons taped to the windows looked down at us with greedy smiles, at the platters of chocolate cupcakes and tubs of goldfish crackers evenly spaced on a row of card tables. The television was on mute. Characters mouthed their lines. It looked like an old episode of *Time Tombs*.

"Birchin," he greeted me.

Birchin was his other daughter, my half-sister, a Republican state representative in Sacramento. We'd never met. Occasionally I read something horrific she'd said in the newspaper.

"Did you see the church?" he asked.

"No. It's me, Petra."

"It's not really a church. Just some chairs and a table. I thought you might like to pray while you're here."

"I'm an atheist. It's Saturday, by the way. Is the wheelchair part of the costume?"

He lifted his leg and pulled back the robe. Thick bandages covered his feet.

"They have to use a machine to get me in and out. A strap," he motioned to his waist. "Like a crane."

I nodded. He was a very large man.

"I'm going to cut the strap," he said. "Then, we'll sue them when I fall. You and your mother can have some money."

"Dad, I'm not Birchin. What happened to your feet?"

"They handed out costumes," he said, tugging on the robe. "We're having a party."

"Your feet," I insisted.

"Charcot."

"What's Charcot?"

He shrugged.

"I remember you were a newscaster for Halloween," he said, adding, "So cute. Most people will be ghosts."

"I never went as a newscaster."

I scrolled my phone, looking for information about Charcot, finding several images of misshapen feet and other diabetic outcomes.

"You did. I made a television set out of cardboard and you stood inside it and broadcast the six o'clock news. You used a wooden spoon for the microphone."

"That wasn't me."

He looked at me strangely, as if I were abandoning a shared con.

"Hypocrites," he said bitterly. "Do as they say, not as they do."

A man leaning on his walker clacked through the open doors on the other side of the room, dressed as Frankenstein, and an anxious nurse stuttered behind him, taking several short steps forward, then half as many back, not so much to hurry him but rather to show us that she could go faster if it weren't for him. She gave us a bubbly, exasperated smile.

"I hate that man," my father said. "I'd like to chop his head off."

"It says you could lose your foot if you have Charcot," I said, waving my phone at him. "Sometimes they have to amputate."

"That'd make you happy."

"No."

"Why are you even here, Birchin?"

"Jesus, Dad. It's Petra. I'm Petra."

"To taunt me? That's what the nurses are for. They cackle at me. Why don't you tell me about Paul? Or what are you doing about the caravan? Tell me about your mother. Distract me. Can't you pretend?"

"I'm not Birchin."

"I know," he growled. "I know exactly who you are."

Residents trickled into the common room one at a time, most of them dressed as ghosts. Their eyes scanned the room for something to magnetize them, the cupcakes, an unfinished puzzle of a snowed-in house, the television set, a corner. One of the women hunched over. When I see people like that,

I feel a compulsion to straighten their spines. It's a terrible idea, of course, they're irreparable, but the feeling is so urgent that maybe I should've been a chiropractor.

"OK, fine. I'm going to a party tonight," I said, turning back to my father. "It's a costume party, which is kind of funny because I don't go to parties and I'm pretending to be someone who does. One of the people at the office invited me. His name is Travis. He's much younger than me. I'm trying not to think about it. Just go, right? I don't have many friends yet. It's been six months so it's time to do something about that. I never went as a newscaster. I went as Janis Joplin. That was my costume. And Paul is Birchin's husband, not mine. Though I can't tell if you're making fun of me, about Mom, and if it's on purpose or unconscious. I don't have to come here, by the way, if that's what you'd prefer. I'm just trying to do what other people do, what people who have fathers do."

He looked down at the scythe.

"Is this all?" he asked me, or maybe himself? I wasn't sure. "Is this all you've become?"

I must've left the car unlocked because someone had put the raccoons behind the steering wheel. They looked like they might snap out of death and drive. However long ago, they'd been darting through the woods, scratching, scarfing food, making all sorts of animal decisions. Now their bodies were locked out of time. Of course, I shouldn't have bought them, but they weren't selling taxidermy statues of my mother. I flung the raccoons onto the backseat with all the other shrapnel of my existence—coffee cups, fast food wrappings, parking receipts, and an old bra I'd used as an oil rag—and headed to the freeway.

Once upon a time, Janis Joplin lived on Ashbury. I know it's adolescent but it's one of the reasons I decided on San Francisco. I dressed like her in middle school and not just for Halloween. I definitely didn't move there for my father. He was a coincidence the way the Golden Gate Bridge was a coincidence—I knew I'd see it, and maybe with some frequency, but it's hardly why I came. At the time, there were a lot of jobs in the Bay Area. I didn't have much in the way of skills except for waitressing, and a firing squad had more appeal than that, so I found admin work at a big soulless accounting firm where most people were half my age.

Freedom's just another word for nothing left to lose.

When I got back to my apartment, a not very cheap derelict studio way out in the Sunset, there was a letter from my ex-husband's mother, written in her mannered cursive. We still corresponded regularly. I wrote one letter for every three of hers.

It was how we kept track of our scorn.

"I ran into the librarian the other day," she wrote, "the one who reminds you of wheat germ. I don't know why you're always saying that. Yes, she's dowdy but I suspect it's because she's lesbian. She's still holding the guide to Costa Rica for you. Shall I tell her to let it go? I suppose there's no convincing you to return. It saddens me, what you said in your letter, that there's nothing here for you anymore, however true that may be. Good Shepherd Presbyterian will be opening its doors again soon. Perhaps you'll come back just for a visit. I'm sure there are good churches out west. Are there? I encourage you to attend a regular service. That's important. Don't lose track of what's important. Do you remember the swizzle stick candies at the antique store on Leonard Road? Would you believe they stopped selling them? It's a crying shame. There is simply no reason to set foot in there any longer. I'm certainly not in the market for an overpriced lamp. What else can I tell you? The rolls at Cumberland's are getting dry. They must've changed bakers. Well, there's a brilliant idea right there. I could speak with Mr. Cumberland if you like. I'm sure he'd be happy to hire you."

Most self-help books lead you to believe there's a single underlying issue and if you can figure it out, you'll be fine. I think it's more like layered mazes. The letter went on for several pages but I had the party to prepare for. I cut a piece of felt, sewed it to the front of the jumpsuit and painted whiskers onto my cheeks. There was no time for a tail. I skipped eating too. There'd be food at the party—famous last words, obviously.

Forest Hill was fifty blocks away. Frenzied trick-or-treaters ran through the streets, forming heavy clots in front of the houses distributing candy. At West Portal, a live zombie band played "I Put a Spell on You" underneath a ragged catering tent. Dancing harpies and undead hockey players spun and twirled, their eyes gleaming in the narcotic lights of the city. Usually, I resented anything that emphasized my loneliness but I stayed awhile to listen to the music. The saxophonist was about my age. She played so beautifully. But when I finally looked to see what time it was, to my shock and horror, my phone had died.

I'd never been to Forest Hill. From what I'd remembered of the map, it was a neighborhood of concentric circles and the party was on the innermost ring. I didn't see anyone on the streets. No trick-or-treaters. No dogwalkers. Not even a car. All the houses looked the same. Quiet black rectangles and triangles. I thought of those smokeless ash trays and how they pull the smoke from the air—the houses seemed to be doing that to sound.

After straggling around for the better part of an hour, I reached a dead end, which is normally the kind of metaphor I heed. My sneakers were old and battered and my feet were tired from walking. But I heard a tinkle of laughter coming from the other side of the trees, so I picked through the brush, gashing my arm badly, actually, but I was so hungry and eager to arrive that I didn't care.

I spilled onto someone's lawn. Cars lined the street in front me, and a trail of jack-o-lanterns led to the front door of a large loud two-story house effervescing with people. I brushed past them and went inside, scanning the room for a familiar face, but it was crowded and everyone was in costume. I went into the kitchen, where it was quieter and brighter, and there was a platter of devils on horseback, thank God. I snapped up several of those and quickly drank a cup of wine.

Next to me, a shirtless, painted blue merman chatted with a lion and a berserker. His long, artfully shaped tail, constructed out of tulle and iridescent scales, swished behind him, shedding blue and purple glitter onto the floor. The lioness was as impressive. She wore a seamless bodysuit with claws and fangs that looked jarringly real—it was hard to tell where the costume began and she ended. For a moment, the berserker, wrapped in goat pelts, regarded me with soulless painted black eyes. The three of them were unfamiliar, and I must've been unfamiliar to them—either that or they were being superior.

The rowdy nests of conversations in the main room called to me. In the closest corner, a glistening golden pharaoh chatted with an expired milk carton barfing up curd. A lemon cello at the center of the room barked at a balding man in a wine-colored toga rolling a massive papier-mâché boulder toward a doorway. A weeping glacier laughed with a woman covered head to toe in rearview mirrors, and a salmon shoved itself against them. A trio of goblins pointed at them and howled.

As I was admiring everyone's lavish costumes, a man stepped in front of me. He wore a white bunny suit with mirrored John Lennon sunglasses.

"Would you like some ether?" he asked, pointing a plastic squeegee bottle at my face.

"No, thank you," I said.

He lowered his glasses.

"Are you sure?"

I didn't know anything about ether but the man looked menacing. Though maybe it was just water in his spray bottle?

On the far side of the room a man and woman leaned against the wall. He was older-looking and they weren't wearing costumes.

"I see some friends. Excuse me," I said.

As I turned, the man lightly stroked my arm. He wasn't trying to grab me.

"Another time," he said.

The couple turned as I approached them with open palms.

"Guys," I said sanctimoniously. "Come on. Not dressing up?"

"Well, I'm a witch in real life," the woman said. "Halloween is my day to relax and be myself."

"Oh, you dress like a witch every day?"

She raised her eyebrows. "It's not like that," she laughed. "I have to dress like you to blend in. We learned that the hard way."

"But you're…Wait, what do you mean?"

"Ever hear of Salem?"

"I'm Avatar, by the way," the man interrupted, extending his hand.

"An avatar," I confirmed, or tried to confirm.

"No, my name is Avatar," he corrected. "I gave myself the name when I became a fictional character."

"Tonight?"

"Twenty years ago."

"I'm Petra," I said, placing my hand over my heart.

"I went to jury duty once dressed in a black robe," the witch said. "Pointy hat. Broom. What you'd expect me to wear. The judge thought I was being cynical. He kicked me out. Can you believe that? I was like—hey! I'm a real witch!"

"Jury duty," I said, shaking my head.

"Are you supposed to be a cartoon character?" the witch asked. "You look like an orange Snagglepuss."

"No," I smiled. "Someone else."

"How do you know Dawn?"

"I work with Travis. Have you seen him? He invited me to come."

"What's he dressed up as?"

"I don't know."

"Well, it'll be hard to pick him out. We came with Nori," Avatar said. "My daughter. It was her idea to do the black and blue issue."

I looked around, unsure if Nori was a real daughter or a fictional daughter. If she were a real person, was he her real or fictional father? If she were fictional, was she imaginary or had he picked someone at random?

"I don't know the black and blue issue."

"I'm surprised," Avatar said, insulted.

"Hey, why can't witches get pregnant?" the witch asked.

"I don't know. I've never—"

"Because their husbands have hollow weenies!"

I laughed, then stepped away.

I squeezed past some people dressed like cutlery, then stopped before a blonde woman in a bikini kneeling on the floor. She was inhaling from a tube connected to a dented blue canister, and she was covered in scars. They were all over her chest, abdomen, arms, and legs. I couldn't tell if they were real or fake.

"Caught you looking," she said to me, her voice absurdly high from helium.

I nodded.

"Yeah, it's bubble gum," she laughed, gesturing to her bikini. "At the end of the night, we're all going to chew it."

"Great."

She handed me a postcard for an upcoming event called Bondage-a-Go-Go.

"You're coming," she said, jabbing me with her finger.

That she considered me invitation material, well, I was flattered, but I became less pleased with myself after flipping over the postcard and seeing a woman in a cherry red bodysuit pouring milk all over a Doberman Pinscher's head.

As I shoved the postcard into my pocket, I smelled something immediately horrific. A vomitous stench. The woman in the bikini looked at something behind me. I turned to see what it was, and found myself facing a man dressed as a cumbersome, alien-looking plant. Large artichoke-shaped leaves draped from his chest like an opened husk and, from the interior yellow shaft that rose almost to the ceiling, a pair of eyes peered out at me struggling through a paroxysm of nausea.

"If you find me attractive, you might be a carrion beetle," he said.

"Sorry, no," I said, trying to back up, but the woman in the bikini and her canisters hemmed me in.

"Or a flesh fly. You might be a flesh fly. They love the way I smell."

Wreathed around his chest were small, netted bags stuffed with what I guessed were cheese rinds and rotting meat. The main shaft was encrusted with pale gluey strands of what smelled like fetid cabbage. It was worse than any dead decaying carcass. My eyes watered. I started to tremble and felt that animal urge to void myself and flee. The man regarded me. He smiled in a mocking way, like a petulant kid who knocks over your toy and then pretends to be innocent.

"I'm just trying to get pollinated, baby," he said, stepping closer. "I'm a corpse flower, by the way."

I felt sweaty. The room shrank. Everything felt very close, like the things that were one foot away and twenty feet away were the same distance. I fell backward onto the woman's helium canister and crashed onto the ground. Something heavy fell beside me. I heard muffled sounds of confusion and concern. A man was lying beside me. He sucked in his breath and groaned. I waited for a few moments. I wasn't sure if I got to my feet that I wouldn't fall right back down. I wondered if I'd hit my head. I looked over at the man. His glasses had broken and the temple was now poking out of his face, with blood running across the bridge of his nose.

"I'm sorry," I whispered.

Someone helped me to my feet. I looked down at the man, who was wearing a brown tweed suit and a sticker on the lapel that said, "Hello, my name is James Joyce." He was very short. I couldn't help noticing that. He touched his nose and looked at his finger while I wondered if I'd gotten it wrong, his size, though I never took my eyes off him. I felt a hand on my arm.

"You alright, honey?"

It was the woman in the bikini. Her voice was normal again, almost brusque.

"Tell Dawn," someone in the crowd said.

"Call 911," someone else said.

A woman dressed as Guinevere knelt beside the man. She tore a piece of fabric from her dress and dabbed at the blood.

"Don't take it out," she cautioned. "Not yet."

"I'm really sorry," I said to him.

"Usurper," he smiled.

I backed into a hallway. It led past a room with stray exercise equipment, then another room with two desks pushed against each other, both covered in stacks of paper. At the end of the hallway, I came to a bathroom with matte black walls and a gilded gold mirror. Cut honeysuckle in a vase leaned against the rim. I washed my face with lemon soap, and that's when it hit me—because the bathroom looked like a hotel bathroom, and the soap was too expensive.

I was at the wrong party.

I locked the door and sat on the edge of the bathtub. I wondered if Travis had sent me there as a joke, or if there really was another party on the inner ring. I could go out and search for it. But that seemed like an extraordinary thing to do. I was tired. And I was already at a party. Did it matter which one?

I went back to the living room. There were more beasts and fewer spaces between them. I didn't see James Joyce, Guinevere, the corpse flower, the Ether Bunny, Avatar, the witch, or anyone from before. It was as if a new crowd had traded places with the old. Like one of those hidden walls had rotated 180 degrees and everyone from before was on the other side now.

I pushed my way into the kitchen. A pair of fawns patted me on the back. One of them offered me a joint. I poured myself some wine instead. Beside me stood a man heaped with leaves and branches, and underneath he wore a camouflage shirt, jacket, and pants—the fire kind, the ice kind, and the purple kind.

"Man versus nature," he acknowledged.

He was talking with Avatar and the witch.

"I want you to imagine something," Avatar said. "And I don't mean this as a sex thing. So please don't take it that way. It's just something I think about when I'm at a shopping mall or a baseball game. A crowded place. What if everyone were naked? What if we were all doing the same thing we normally do—buying things, talking to each other, stopping at the food court, laughing or, at the game, pitching, catching, the third-base coach signaling for a bunt down the line—but naked?"

"That's what you're supposed to do when you're nervous," the witch said. "When you're addressing a crowd. Imagine everyone is naked."

"No, that's different. That's about power. This is anthropological. This is about restoring a vision of ourselves as we truly are, in our modern age."

The man in leaves gestured to himself and nodded.

"Without the invention of adornment," he added.

"Aren't there still nudist colonies?" I asked.

"What?"

"Nudist colonies. People go there for vacations. Or maybe people live there full time. I don't know. They used to do reports about them on *20/20* and shows like that. Don't those still exist?"

"That's not what I'm talking about at all," Avatar resisted. "It has to be everyone, everywhere. Nudists live in exile. I'm talking about a figure skating competition, and it's everyone in the crowd, the judges, the announcers, the skaters, the people at the concession stand, and all the people walking around the stadium, people driving taxis, people at home, people in airplanes."

"It'd give you a glimpse," I said.

"If there's a place on Earth where someone is still wearing clothes, then no, it wouldn't give you a glimpse. It'd be a distortion," he said adamantly.

"Adornment has yet to be invented, is that right?" the man in eucalyptus leaves asked.

"I love this so much," the witch said. "It's like Adam and Eve in the garden, but the garden is the Oakland Colosseum and there's no original sin."

"Yes, but the garden is everywhere. I can't emphasize that enough. We go to appointments at the bank and the supermarket and everyone is naked in every country."

"And it's not a sex thing," the witch reminded me.

"Though sex would be interesting," the man in leaves said. "As a man attempts to return to the womb, or the grave, as the case may be, and the woman is engorged—"

Someone grabbed my shoulder.

"Is your name Petra?"

It was a woman in a magenta body suit, my age, with round amphetamine blue eyes.

"Yes," I said, bewildered—for a moment I thought I'd come to the right place after all.

"I can't believe it. Petra Schoen. What are the odds?"

"Sorry, I don't recognize you," I admitted.

"Missy Malone. From Maryland. We went to the same school. Do you work on the magazine?"

"Missy Malone."

"You remember," she said, though it was more of a command.

"OK. Yeah. You were in the senior play. Right?"

"No worries. It's been thirty years, I probably look like a completely different person. Have you lived here this whole time?

"Just six months."

"Good for you. I came for law school. Got married. To Jeff. Remember Jeff? We have two teenagers. And a Burmese Mountain dog named Rheingold. Jeff likes the beer. You look the same, by the way."

"Is that good?"

"You remember Jeff."

"Was he in the play?"

"You remember him. It'd be a little weird if you didn't. We didn't go to a big school. I'll show you a picture."

She began scrolling. Her son, from what I saw, looked menacing, with long hair and large hands, and her industrial-gothic daughter had the face of a bollard.

"Do you have kids?" she asked.

I didn't answer. She didn't notice. She was too focused on her phone, flashing through images of her dog before finally landing on one of Jeff, a whatever-looking guy, the kind of generic upper-middle class person who said, despite having received every break in life, "You make your own luck."

"You remember him."

Out of the corner of my eye I saw the corpse flower hunched under the doorway. No one was paying attention to him or bristling at the smell. I wondered if everyone was used to it. Maybe I'd overreacted. I shielded myself behind Missy but the corpse flower spotted me and started to approach. I drank my wine, thinking of 10th grade science class when I slit a footlong worm with an Exacto blade. I felt a strong desire to run a knife down the corpse flower's shaft and spill its jellied kerosene insides onto the floor.

"Petra?" Missy asked. "Do you remember?"

"Yes," I said. "Totally."

"Hey, you look pale. Was it that bad? People are always telling me all the horrible things he did."

"No, I'm fine."

"I'll get you some water," she said, turning.

But the corpse flower stood in her way. It seemed taller now. The top of the shaft folded against the ceiling. Maybe the living room ceiling was taller. Or maybe the corpse flower had grown. I shrank from the smell.

"If you find me attractive," the corpse flower said to Missy, "you might be a carrion beetle."

"I'm going," I said.

"But we haven't done the ceremony yet," Missy said, grabbing my arm.

"I'm not supposed to be here," I said.

"Or a flesh fly," the corpse flower said. "You might be a flesh fly."

I pulled my arm but Missy grabbed it again.

"Stay," she said.

"Come with me," I countered.

She handed me the wine bottle and smiled. We shoved our way past the corpse flower and burst out the door.

Or at least I thought we did.

Missy had remained inside.

I wandered from the house and up the winding streets until I came to a four-lane road straddling the edge of the hill. A chain-link fence held the ledge, and bits of fabric knotted to the tension wire fluttered in the wake of the cars. I stopped to read a torn anarchist manifesto stapled to a telephone pole. Another lost cat with little hope of returning. I looked to the south. The sentimental orange lights twinkled. I tried to imagine what Avatar had imagined, everyone naked, all the people in their living rooms, in the cars coming by, at the party, at my father's nursing home, in the mirror, *to see ourselves as we really are.*

"Pretend I'm not here," I thought.

The four-lane road spiraled down into a residential neighborhood at the bottom of the hill. By then I'd become aware of a terrible blister growing at the back of my heel. I didn't see any taxis, my phone was still dead, and I was starving. I walked for a long time past candy color houses and all the cars parked along the street. I stopped to pick my ankle in front of a lawn full of skeletons arranged in pairs. They were having sex, I realized, or made to look like they were having sex, their jaws open in macabre ecstasy.

I found a bar called Embers on a street corner. It was one of those nowhere places strung with Christmas lights. Photos of regulars covered the mirror behind the bar. I drank a beer and ate pretzels from a wooden salad bowl. They were showing World Series highlights on a television in the corner, and one of Birchin's campaign ads came on. Last year, someone had thrown a shoe at her at a police officer's funeral. The police never identified the assailant but Birchin claimed he was an illegal immigrant, then designed her entire campaign around the slogan "California can't wait for the other shoe to drop."

I often wondered if she'd staged the attack.

I took my drink to the back, where a few young men were playing pool. I sat down to watch, mollified by the slow monotony of the game and the balls cracking against each other. At the next table, two old men in burgundy suits talked and laughed. They told each other dirty jokes. They must've been about seventy. It took me a while to realize they were identical twins.

It was nice just to listen and to watch.

I finished a second beer and left.

A bride of Frankenstein, an impertinent nurse, Smurfette, and a clan of forest animals were all kneeling around a silver station wagon outside the bar. The bride was skidding candy underneath and the nurse murmured and pointed. The bride appeared to grow frustrated and began sliding larger packages of candy instead of individual pieces. I could feel everyone tighten in anticipation. Suddenly, a family of raccoons burst from underneath the station wagon. There were four of them. The nurse screamed. The forest animals cheered and chased after them but the raccoons had chugged off into the darkness. The bride leaned back on her hands and laughed.

Before moving to San Francisco, I often called my mother on the phone. The first time, a man answered. He had a heavy Eastern European accent and was very nice. He said it was OK to leave messages, but a month later, an orthodontist's office took over the number. They used an automated system, which exposed the charade. A year later, the number switched hands again and for a long time I got an answering machine with no outgoing message. It just clicked and signaled that it was recording. That made it much easier to imagine my mother was getting my messages.

Walking home from the bar, I decided to call her. I took out my phone. It was dead, of course. I'd forgotten that. But I could pretend to call her, I realized. I was already pretending.

To my surprise, she picked up.

"Mom?"

"Petra. It's so good to hear your voice. What are you doing?"

"Nothing, really. Walking home. I just left a party. A costume party. It's Halloween. And I saw Dad. He was dressed as the Grim Reaper."

"He was at the party?"

"No. I saw him earlier. At the nursing home. I don't think I'll go back there anymore. You know, I'm almost fifty now. What's the point, right? We're practically strangers."

"He left us, Petra. He turned his back on us."

"I mean, we don't really have a relationship. I've tried to manufacture one. I go there and sit beside him, ask him how he's feeling, try to help him with medical stuff or getting him better pillow sheets or magazines, because I don't want him to feel so alone. But half the time he pretends I'm his other daughter and the other half he really believes I'm her. And I'm not sure which is which. You know what I mean?"

"Yes, I think so."

"Did I ever dress up as a TV reporter for Halloween, by the way?"

"No."

"Sometimes I go so the staff won't abuse him. If they think someone cares about him maybe they won't abuse him. That's a real thing you never had to deal with."

"Lucky me."

"Good one."

"What would it be like if you didn't try?" she asked. "If you went to see him and didn't make any effort?"

"I don't get the point. We'd just sit there."

"Yes."

"Saying nothing."

"Maybe."

"Are you trying to tell me something and make me think it's my idea?"

"I'm just asking."

"If I'm not trying to help him, then there's nothing. It's just a void."

"Or."

"Or what?"

"Or it's a fresh place to start."

"Two random people could do that. Strangers could do that. Or maybe that's what you mean. That we're strangers?"

"You must be getting something out of it."

"No."

"No?"

"No."

"OK, then."

"Maybe I should've stayed in Maryland. At least I had a book club there. I didn't have to deal with Dad."

"Joining a book club in San Francisco is the absolute minimum thing you could do. I don't know why you haven't done that yet. Or why you're chasing young men at your job. Or dealing with your father. No one is asking you to do any of that."

"I don't want to join a book club."

"You want a pity party."

"No."

"You want a relationship with your father."

"Isn't that a natural thing to want?"

"What do you mean?"

"It's like saying you want air to breathe, you want food to eat. Everybody wants those things."

"But he left us. It was just you and me."

"Mom."

"What?"

"Stop."

"Stop what?"

"Pretending."

"Pretending what?"

"Pretending like you know what I should do all the time."

"I'm not."

"Yes, you are."

"No."

"You're not even talking right now. You're pretending."

"I am talking to you right now."

"No, you're not."

"What am I doing then?"

"Making fun of me."

"Oh, Petra."

"What?"

"I'm trying to help. You're just too…"

"Too what?"

"I don't know. I just wish you could be with me now."

"No."

"Lying next to me, feeling my warm breath on the back of your neck."

"Stop."

"Falling asleep next to me with your hands scrunched in your sweater and me holding you and caressing you."

"Stop it."

"Shush, shush, shush…"

"Stop," I yelled. "Stop."

About two years later, my father died. His heart stopped during the night. I had no reason to suspect the nurse of lying, other than the image of a peaceful death was better for the nursing home business. I guess I wanted my father to pay for what he'd done, and because payment is made through pain, I imagined several scenarios in which he'd suffered—the nurse, for example, smothering him with a pillow while we spoke on the phone.

I'd only seen him once more, after driving home from a job interview in Sebastopol. I wasn't his other daughter anymore, I was anyone, he was anyone. We mostly talked about food.

Cemeteries are something I'd like to better understand—specifically, how they keep finding places to bury people. There's a never-ending supply of bodies and cemeteries have a fixed area, like parking lots, but parking lots get full, and cemeteries don't. There are probably some facts I don't really want to know. In the city, parking garages have these lifts that can stack the cars. Maybe cemeteries had something similar underground.

Birchin and her mother had arranged the funeral. They greeted me and the other guests beside a trellis woven with chrysanthemums.

"So good of you to come," the mother said, taking my hand.

I sat down on a metal folding chair. There were about a hundred people dressed in customary black attire. I didn't recognize any of them. I had the feeling they were there for Birchin and not my father. The priest spoke first. He accused my father of being "a loyal foot soldier in God's army" and that he "never shillyshallied in his faith." What was funny is that it might've been true. Maybe my father was religious and I never even knew that.

Birchin spoke next. She gave her eulogy in the unexpected form of a crossword, reading a clue and then telling us the story behind it. Apparently, my father loved doing crosswords. Every year he designed a puzzle just for her, containing clues only she could answer, things from her childhood or private jokes they shared, and gave it to her on her birthday. When she got to nine across, "pet name," she stooped forward and her hair spilled over the lectern. She grabbed the sides to steady herself. I saw that she was shaking. She loved him. She loved him with the most natural sincerity. It may sound stupid but it'd never occurred to me that they loved each other.

That they actually had love.

Afterward, I wandered through the cemetery. I read the names and dates on many of the tombstones. Many people had left behind flowers or framed photographs that faded in the sun, but most of the graves looked ragged. I wondered what would happen to my father's, would I ever come back, or would Birchin visit him each Sunday with a crossword puzzle.

About fifty yards away, a woman was kneeling in front of a grave marker, moving her hands in circles through the grass. A young boy, maybe three or four years old, strayed behind her. He jumped from stone to stone, tugged at grass blades, and crept further away while she grieved. A black hearse pulled onto the bypass road in the distance. It was moving fast. The boy wandered down into the furrow by the side of the road. I could see the angles lining up, so I started to run. The boy was just stepping onto the road as the hearse came over the crest. I grabbed the boy and pulled him down. The hearse sped by. The boy shouted and began to sob. His mother ran over. She held out her arms to take him.

"Oh my god," she cried. "Thank God. Thank God you were here. Thank God."

Big Sur

Her father drove north on Highway 5. Most of the time she stared out the window. She saw cows clustered on hills of blonde grass, dead tractors, black birds dozing on power lines. An eighteen-wheeler with a colorless Minnie Mouse tied to the front passed them on the right. Her father focused on the road, one hand slung over the steering wheel, the other on the gearshift. They couldn't agree on a radio station so she turned down the volume and left it on Seek.

Whenever she looked at him, his face seemed old and heavy, and she felt sorry for him, because he was old and heavy. They were different, of course, but that was obvious. She had his nose and not much else. When he'd picked her up that morning, she was lying on the cowhide rug in her dorm room, tracing her finger over the "N" and the "I" branded into the cow's skin. Her mind had wandered into a world where cows bought human skins and laid them onto their living room floors.

Besides a burger, what was a cow inside.

"I heard a story on the radio last night," her father said. "About two guys in the Yukon."

Chewing on her thumbnail, she took too much and winced. She sucked on it, tasting pennies. In *Romeo and Juliet*, it was an insult to bite your thumb but that always seemed so random. At least when you gave someone the finger, it had an obvious etymology. Maybe back in the day biting your thumb was like vagina dentata.

"Is the Yukon really a place?" she asked.

"Yes, it's in Canada."

"But do they really call it the Yukon? That's not a Jack London thing?"

"They were building an igloo together," he continued. "They were almost done. They just needed to do the top. The guy on the inside was bald and it was getting warm inside so he took off his hat. He popped his head out to ask the other guy a question, but when the other guy saw his bald head poke out of the hole, he instinctively smashed it in with his ice axe."

"That's horrible."

Her father glanced over his shoulder before changing lanes.

"You know there are mirrors," she said.

"You know there are blind spots," he said.

"Why'd you tell me that story?"

"Seemed like your cup of tea."

When she was very young, she pretended to be a dog, a frog, a bunny, a dolphin, and when her parents asked her, "Are you a dog? A frog? A bunny? A dolphin?" she answered, "No. No. No. No." When her baby teeth came out, her mother snuck quarters under her pillow while she pretended to be asleep. When she was in first grade her teacher gave her chocolate milk during snack time and she pretended to be ambivalent. When she was twelve she smeared ketchup on her neck as if her throat had been slashed and waited on the living room floor for her parents to discover her.

They exited the highway and drove west. Near King City they stopped at El Rey for lunch at Macho Nacho like they did every year. The boy at the counter had a glistening faux hawk. His cheeks were covered in archipelagos of acne. She ordered a Tecate and while they waited for their food, she drank her beer combatively. On the walls were a dozen paintings of the same long-haired warrior carrying the same unconscious princess.

"I have an idea," she said. "Let's not do this next year."

They arrived at Big Sur an hour before sunset. Her father parked between two black SUVs. He collected his things from the backseat while she hopped out and lit a Camel Light. She looked for the man inside the camel's front leg. Some people thought he had an erection. Some people thought he was Mae West. Her roommate said the man was getting a blowjob from a woman on her hands and knees while she was being fucked by a lion. Her father handed her a bundle of white roses wrapped in brown paper. He tucked a second one under his arm.

"Smoking," he said.

A long flight of stairs led to the beach, where a group of late afternoon picnickers sat on an oversized blanket. At the shore, ragged rocks broke the waves. A five-year-old lorded over a tide pool.

At the water's edge, she gave her father a weak smile. He returned it, but his face was more solemn. She imagined his face molded into a mask for her to wear, and then she imagined her face with a less solemn expression, turning that into a mask for him. The masks were not to be worn over the face, they were to be worn on the inside, like a secret face.

Side by side they unwrapped their bundles. She placed her flowers into the water and he did the same. The roses bowed under the waves. The process was slow, the surf churned the petals and stems and carried them away. The sky darkened. Somehow she was holding his hand. She didn't remember reaching for it. There was a time when there was no difference between them, when she was him, they were actually in the same body.

The beach behind them was abandoned. The picnickers were gone but they'd left behind their blanket.

"We don't have to go to Macho Nacho anymore," he said.

"No. It's tradition."

"It's disgusting."

She laughed.

"It is disgusting," she agreed.

At the stairwell, a pair of gutterpunks met them on the steps. One had the sides of his head shaved. The rest of his hair was clipped with barrettes. The other was tall, too young for wounds.

"Spare a dollar?" they asked.

Before she could say no, her father was already in his wallet. He surrendered a ten-dollar bill. The boys bowed in sarcastic gratitude. At the top of the stairs, she imagined picking up a truck and throwing it down on them. She pictured them crushed under the weight of the truck and their insides spilling out like cockroach blood.

As they walked back to the car, she glowered at her father. His face was bruised with shadows.

Typically, they stayed at Karp's, but it'd burned down that winter. So they looked for a place near Carmel. She was surprised he hadn't booked something in advance. She'd liked staying at Karp's. The painter Patrick Nagel had lived there for some time and the lobby was hung with many of his paintings. It was how he'd paid rent.

She'd often smoked pot outside and then came back in to look at the paintings while her father slept. The images were so melodramatic, the cocaine-skinned models with jet-black hair wearing yellow triangle earrings or a swatch of turquoise. The paintings were cartoonish fantasies, desperately erotic, ridiculous permissions.

The desk clerk at Karp's had been a heavy man whose face resembled an uncomfortable cushion. He'd worn a pencil-drawn goatee around his small mouth.

"I have two of his paintings in my room, if you'd like to see them," he said.

She imagined his penis, that it looked like someone who goes to a party and stands around waiting for the night to end, as if the whole point of the party was for everyone else to feel indignant that this person came at all, uninvited. With a seam that ran down the middle of the scrotum, as if sewn by hand. As if it were a sad alien fruit.

It felt good to know when someone was asking for sex.

The women in the paintings often looked like they were making a pass at you from across the room at an expensive party. They were extravagantly posed against grids or monochromatic shapes, petting a leopard, sometimes removing a bit of clothing, almost always meeting someone's gaze. One exception on the far wall was of a woman squatting with her back to the viewer. She wore a kamikaze headband and sandals and her eyes were cast downward, as if contemplating some unknowable disappointment.

As far as she knew, Patrick Nagel had only painted women. She didn't know what he looked like. A man in a white suit, probably. A man holding his paintbrush in one hand and his dick in the other. His paintings were mirrors. The man at the front desk had told her Nagel died young. She didn't know if he'd painted live models but she thought it would be fun to meet him and smoke a joint with him and pose for a painting.

"What should I do?" she would've asked him.

"Just be yourself," he would've said.

An M has two legs and a phallus. A W is two sagging breasts. An M is for man but also for mother. A W is for woman but also for whatever.

That semester, she'd taken an art class with a student named Richard Bonds. For their last assignment, Richard built a very large motorized contraption out of metal and wool. Two long arms extended from the base and were fitted with harnesses. The purpose of the machine was to bring the arms together like two hands clapping. A gas generator provided power.

Richard put up fliers around the school, inviting everyone to the courtyard near his studio. He set up his machine there, and he attached to one of the arms a reproduction of Gustave Courbet's *Origin of the World*, which he'd rendered himself. After the crowd assembled, Richard removed his clothes and strapped himself to the other arm. He clicked a remote control and the machine began to slap him and the painting together.

Whenever she looked at the original *Origin of the World*, the Rorschach test of pubic hair dragged her eye down. She always stared at the crevice, forgetting the subject's face, the fact that she didn't have one. Eventually she decided that the painting wasn't about women. And it wasn't about how men desired women or truth or birth. It was about how men saw themselves.

When the machine stopped slamming Richard and the painting together, he unstrapped himself and stumbled forward, his face and chest scraped and bleeding. He slipped on a robe that was waiting for him on a foldout chair and limped into the closest building while the crowd walked away in disgust.

She went over to the machine. The canvas was coming off the stretcher bars. She flipped it over and spread it out on the lawn. Because the paint hadn't dried, it all smeared together during the performance. It looked like molasses and butter and blood. What had been pubic hair now bloomed in a dark molestation. There was no body anymore. There was no more woman.

It occurred to her, as her father pulled into the Holiday Inn Express parking lot, that there were two different tribes, a Holiday Inn tribe and a Holiday Inn Express tribe, but she didn't know the difference. Were there even regular Holiday Inns anymore? Had the Express tribe won?

In the hotel lobby, she listened to three women buzzing about how much cheesecake they'd devoured at dinner.

"I shouldn't have," one of them pretended to confess.

The women were not her tribe.

After booking their rooms with the desk clerk, who concealed his contempt with a robotic obsequiousness, they walked to the elevator.

"Do you remember in sixth grade there was a boy who sent me roses?" she asked.

"Yes," he said.

"Did you know I kicked him in the nuts?"

"No. What? Why?"

"We were doing a séance at Kelly Kessler's house. We took turns lying on the rug. Everyone put two fingers under the person's body and lifted them up. When it was Jonah's turn—"

"Jonah was the one who sent you flowers?"

She nodded.

"When he closed his eyes, I kicked him in the nuts. I kicked him as hard as I could."

"Did it feel good?"

"For him?"

"For you."

He pressed the button for the third floor. She saw that he was still wearing his wedding ring, which was crushing on two levels. One, obviously, get over it. And two, wedding rings were gross. No one ever acknowledged the symbolism of the finger going into the circle. Like unicorn horns and neckties were penises. At her summer internship a woman there had gotten engaged and was showing off her ring. Everyone was gabbling and praising her while all she could do was think how a diamond was just an obnoxious crystalline clit.

"You know, it's not easy for anyone," her father said, handing her the key card to her room.

She went inside and sat down at the edge of the bed. Above the headboard, there was a painting of a landscape so unremarkable that no one would be able to point it out in a police lineup. She watched the ceiling fan cut the air like a star hurtling in place.

Hours later, she woke up in the bathtub with her arm flopped over the side and her clothes puddled on the floor.

She didn't remember taking them off. She didn't remember getting into the tub. The last thing she remembered was the joint. Lighting it, the flame enveloping the tip like a valiant orange foreskin. She'd blown the smoke into the sink to conceal the smell. Only a few images from the night's slideshow lingered—her mother's hazel eyes, George Washington's face on the dollar bill, algae, each image transforming into the other.

As she rose from the tub, she looked at her naked self. She scanned her chest, her stomach, her genitals, the ash of her knees. She made a sound like a terrified balloon.

Sometimes you're reading a book or magazine and you scan over "really" but really it's "reality." Sometimes the word you see is wound. And then suddenly you have to push shit through your ear. Suddenly your heart is your tongue. Suddenly blood fountains in your throat. But your eyes are the same dark clots. Under your lip is the same scar from when a boy cut your mouth with scissors. The folds in your cheeks are like your face was made of ham. That hasn't changed. Your face is the same. It's not a penis face the way some people have a penis face, with dented foreheads, veined skin, jutting jawbones, coarse hair, eyes spaced too wide apart. But even though your face is the same, you're not the same. You're an undesirable putrescent gray.

She wondered what her body would look like. A murder costume. She imagined the blood. Her father would have to see her like that. They would tell him that she was dead. She was a witch. A witch who didn't mourn enough. At the Palisades she once hiked to the top of a giant waterfall. At the top, she wanted to leap into the chasm. She told her then-boyfriend she felt suicidal.

"No, that's just gravity calling you," he'd laughed.

She thought of walking into traffic. Stepping in front of a car. A car filled with black balloons. Black starlings flying into the air. Some people were always getting rid of themselves. Parents taught their children to believe their toes were pigs.

Hurriedly she put on her clothes and ran down the back stairwell.

She decided to go to Karp's, to see if there was anything left of the Nagels. She thought of those unhappy people who say, "Everything happens for a reason." That never quite rang true to her. And then, maybe after Karp's, she'd return to Big Sur and look for the white roses they'd tossed into the sea.

Mobile phone stores and bank branches flanked the sides of the street. She walked past a man in a yellow jacket and baggy chinos. A plastic bag stuffed with wet newspapers hung from his hand. It took her an hour to find the old Karp's lot. It was mostly rubble and a few stray black boards. Someone had left behind a green baseball hat that was brighter than any of the weeds. She found small oddities like a zipper handle from a suitcase and metal cufflinks. There was also a rusty dumpster filled with burned mattresses. She picked up a stick and walked around with it.

An hour passed before her father appeared.

He slammed the door of his car.

"What the fuck are you doing? Why haven't you answered your phone?"

She thought of pretending to be dead. They'd ignored her when she'd covered herself in ketchup. She hadn't wanted to be dead, she'd wanted to be acknowledged, so that's what they deprived her of.

"I wanted to see if anything was left."

"Seriously, what is wrong with you?" he pressed.

He didn't wait for an answer. Instead he got up and fetched two water bottles from the car. He drank them both before coming back to her. She took out a cigarette but he snatched it out of her mouth.

"You have to talk," he said. "You have to talk to me."

Instead she drew in the dirt with her finger, carving not quite letters.

"That doesn't say anything," he said.

"I had a terrible dream," she finally said. "We were back at the beach at Big Sur and you were…"

"What?"

"I don't want to say."

"I'm not—"

"You were making me have sex with you," she said.

Her father looked strangely neutral.

"I was behind you and you were on your knees. You kept curling your arm around me. You kept hooking me in. Your back was paste. Like, literally paste, but with bleeding scrapes on it."

"That was your dream last night?"

"No, last month."

"What else?"

"That's not enough?" she bristled.

"If we're going to try and understand it—"

"I don't want to understand it."

"Then why tell me about it?"

"Because I don't know what else to say."

He kicked dirt onto the almost letters.

She looked at him accusingly. He'd been all of her, then half of her, then none of her, and yet she was still trapped inside him, in some bullshit world, not hers, one she could never escape from and all its lurid disguises and humiliations.

She gathered her arms around her knees and looked at the cars, and the dumpster, at the sky, anywhere but him. There were clouds crossing above her. One of them resembled a bird, she thought, but soon it pulled apart, it lost its wings and talons and turned into a cloud.

The Necessity of Dark Places to Transact a Dark Business

I read my mother's notebooks after she died. She'd written about my father obsessively, in an almost gothic poetry, about how he'd manipulated her into having sex. Yet she'd claimed the domination was somehow hers, that it belonged to her, that it was love. She wrote that he'd had her—that's how she always described it, as having her—until there was nothing left, not even ash.

He was a psychologist. Before they married, my mother was his patient. He was Haitian. She was French. Most people say I'm anybody's guess. They were enough to make me skeptical of therapy. But it didn't matter, I had to go for eighteen weeks, per the sentencing guidelines. A place on the Upper West Side, a brownstone across the street from a police station, as if to prove the farce.

I know everyone goes through phases, but at some point you are who you are. I'm not trying to pretend otherwise. I'd done what they said I did. My body is a kind of condemned material. Condemned to want. Condemned to have, as my mother would say.

Polluted with desire.

When people are turned on, they say, "I want your body." I say that too. But sex is more like I want my body to disappear into yours.

The problem is it never lasts.

Whatever crawls out comes back.

The therapist's place was on West 82nd Street. Next to some trash cans loosely chained to a wrought iron gate, wet newspapers moldered under fallen leaves. Scrolls of peeling paint clung to the brownstone wall near a pair of cats watching me from a second-story window. They were the kind that look like antebellum generals. I don't particularly like cats. I don't think you can use one body part to make your other parts clean.

Someone buzzed me in and I followed a trail of noise machines through a corridor to a large room at the back of the building. A group sat in a circle. They looked at me with casual aversion while Dr. Rieux, a tall, hygienic-looking man in his late fifties, gestured toward an empty metal folding chair.

"Paul," he said. "Welcome."

I took a seat between a bony woman with dyed-red hair and a man stuffed inside a Dartmouth sweatshirt. Across the circle, a woman with bangs offered a diffident wave. A framed print of Matisse's *Dance*, which always seemed smug to me, hung on the wall behind her.

"Would you like to introduce yourself? Maybe just a few words about why you're here," Dr. Rieux asked.

Other than coercion, I didn't know what to expect from therapy. No one in the room looked like a sex addict to me. The women wore plain cardigans and pressed blouses like maybe they had HR jobs. The men resembled dough.

Dr. Rieux nodded.

"Well, I can understand feeling guarded," he said. "We're strangers to you now. But, as I like to say when someone first walks into this room, you're like a crumpled-up ball of paper. We can't tell what's written there. You have to open up so we can learn your story. In a few weeks, we'll be able to read between the lines and tell you things you didn't know about yourself. But first, we need to hear from you."

I had no intention of talking.

A metal chair rasped.

"I'll go if he won't," the woman with dyed-red hair said.

Dr. Rieux lowered his eyes.

"Last night, I was doing the dishes. I heard Frank come in. He didn't say anything, he just started nibbling. Telling me he was harder than a rock. Big fucking deal, you know?"

"You didn't appreciate that," Dr. Rieux acknowledged.

"No. I was thinking about my cousin who just lost her daughter. For

Christ's sake, I was thinking about a dead baby. Frank could care less. He's just there for a transaction. He thinks I'm always turned on."

"Do you regret telling him?"

"You were conflicted," the woman with bangs reminded her.

"I told Frank I was going to Duane Reade but as soon as I left I called Tristan. We went in his gypsy cab to Hunters Point. It was deserted, dark. The first time was good. I should've stopped there but I kept chasing it. He pushed me off at some point. He actually complained, which made me feel stupid, rejected, empty, all those wonderful feelings."

I glanced at her, and pictured her in the car. She was the kind of person you could see the skeleton inside of.

"When I came home," she continued, "Frank was snoring on the couch. His breath kept getting caught in his throat. I thought of going down on him, but instead I masturbated on the floor. I didn't fantasize about him. Or Tristan. Actually, I was thinking that Frank should see a doctor for apnea, and I was thinking about today, wondering what I'd talk about. That's what I was thinking of when I came."

"That's what got you off?" Dr. Rieux asked.

"No," she said. "Well, yes, but it was because I imagined having nothing to say."

The man in the Dartmouth sweatshirt spoke next. He was in the habit of sneaking off to hotels so he could watch pornography without interruption—apparently his wife spent all her time walking around the apartment opening doors. I wasn't sure what to do with that besides picture him, this big precipitative man in his open robe on a bed with a laptop. Same with the woman with dyed-red hair. I could picture her fingertips white against the window of the gypsy cab. Was that how therapy was supposed to work? One person shoveling their problems into another?

After the session, we filed through the corridor. Not completely by accident, I kicked over one of the noise machines, the kind therapists use to suppress whatever their patients say so no one on the outside gets contaminated, and the woman with bangs looked at me in a pained way, as if I'd just released a swarm of deadly black flies.

Outside, a small crowd of black-shirted activists had assembled in front of the police station. They were yelling at a pair of officers who were dragging a woman with pink hair into the station. One of the activists, a tall, skinny man with a curled moustache, charged the officers. Though they deflected the man easily, the scuffle caused the woman to stumble and her pink wig slid off, revealing an open wound above her ear. Many of the activists sagged back, repulsed by the blood, then suddenly they leapt at the officers, who hurried the woman inside the station and barred the door.

I made my way to the Natural History Museum and slumped onto a bench. Across from me sat a man eating a sandwich. He made the mistake of brushing some crumbs off his coat, which summoned several pigeons. They paced at the man's feet, acting like they didn't know there was food. The man waved his arms and the birds fluttered away briefly before resuming their siege.

For a moment, it crystallized for me—the meat in the man's sandwich and the meat in his arm, his knobby wrist bone and the dinosaur bones on display in the museum, the dinosaurs and the birds and how one became the other over time, these very birds had once been pterodactyls, and the man's hunger, the birds' hunger, the woman with dyed-red hair's hunger, the people walking out of the museum looking for lunch's hunger, and the hunger of the minotaur watching them from the bench—an array of mirrors that cracked into so what.

The activists made it onto Columbus and were now coming toward the museum. The curly moustache man carried a chain. On the sidewalk, a young mother pulled her baby from the stroller and pointed at them. She bounced it up and down and talked in its ear. The activists passed and turned onto the driveway that led to the museum and I was sure they'd use the chain to break the glass doors of the atrium. But instead, they just filed inside with the other ticketholders.

I went over to Amsterdam. A sinewy teenager hung from a scaffolding bar and his friend was smoking pot on the curb. They jabbered at me, then the one on the scaffolding followed. I slid into one of those public gardens that occasionally appear between buildings. A man spraying dead leaves dropped the hose and left the garden. I waited a few minutes but the teenager never showed.

Uptown, I found a bar with papered-over windows. A young wisp in a clean white shirt poured me a glass of vodka. I brought it to the back, where a group of students took turns critiquing the police. I had the strange feeling that they were performing for each other, that they didn't really believe the things they said. The content could've been anything. I wondered if it was more of a mating ritual, and the two students who demonstrated the most conviction would win each other's favor and go home together.

Solitary men in flannel shirts drank cocktails out of pint glasses and watched a basketball game from several years ago. Seated underneath a Toulouse-Lautrec print, an Asian woman texted on her phone with one finger while drinking a beer. Her hair was pulled back so tightly that her forehead looked like a rind. I watched her mouth the words she poked into the phone. She looked up and seemed unbothered by my gaze, so I went over to her.

We drank for a couple of hours. She told me her dissertation was about mapping the brains of musicians who were showing early signs of dementia. Under the pretext of having cigarettes at her apartment, we went to her place. She had only one chair, so we sat on the edge of her futon, drinking beer and listening to the radio before finding a way out of our clothes.

In one of her notebooks, my mother wrote that being with my father made her feel like smoke. There were no edges to her feelings or experiences. In a nightmare, he surrounded her in a great black plume, but it wasn't him, it was a chimera made of all the times they'd had sex. My father's interpretation, which she'd documented, was that she was obsessed with annihilation, that this was her darkest desire. My father was a stranger to me. So was his interpretation. I've wondered sometimes if he's just an idea in my head, the way a person's voice is just an idea in your head when you talk to them on the phone, if he never really had a body. I'd lived longer with her notebooks but at least I remember my mother stepping out of the shower with beads of water on her skin.

I skipped therapy for the next three weeks. I stopped going to work. I went to bars instead, burning through money and seeking out strangers. Sometimes I paid for sex. My boss left several messages. My probation officer called too. Unless I went back to therapy, he said, jail was in the cards.

Dr. Rieux made a welcoming gesture upon my return, as if opening the door to a royal chamber, and I took a seat across from two people—a man and a woman—who hadn't been there the first time. From the way they clumped their legs together, they appeared to be a couple.

"I'd like to introduce you all to Arthur and Helena," Dr. Rieux announced.

"We're very grateful to be with you," Arthur said cautiously, as if we were sharing a table at a wedding.

Helena nodded vaguely.

Dr. Rieux turned to me.

"Paul, I wasn't sure you'd be back," he said. "I assume that means you're ready to share."

I shook my head. The woman with dyed-red hair leaned forward on her seat. She wore a plain yellow blouse with rolled up sleeves. I'd misjudged her, I realized. She did look like a sex addict.

Dr. Rieux sighed.

"I understand that you're obligated to attend therapy," he said. "You think you don't need it and you feel like an outsider. So, if you plan to sit here quietly for eighteen weeks, and just be a passenger, maybe you'll see something out the window that resonates with you, and maybe it'll give you some small comfort or a feeling of superiority. But if there's a part of you that can see this as an opportunity to heal, I encourage you to take it."

I scratched my fingers.

"I just don't see the point," I said.

"The point of…?"

"Therapy."

"OK," he said, reaching out his hand for more.

"Let's say I had this terrible thing happen to me. Just as an example, let's say my parents died in a fire when I was young. I come here, tell you all the details, the whole horror movie of my life. I have a catharsis. You're like, cool, we really understand him now, a terrible thing happened to him. It's out in the open. But the problem is I don't have a terrible thing that happened to me. This is just who I am."

"You don't need a terrible thing to be here."

"Then what am I supposed to be healing from?"

"I'd pose that question to you."

"I'm just like this."

"Are you a happy person?" he asked.

"Of course not. What kind of person says they're happy?"

"Let me put it another way. Do you like how you're living? Would you like to change anything if you could?"

"There's nothing wrong with having a lot of sex."

"I agree with that in principle."

"Look, I'm not the one with a problem. The cops are the ones with a problem. They're the fucked-up ones."

"What does having a lot of sex mean to you?"

When I didn't respond, Dr. Rieux turned to the woman with bangs.

"Do you have a lot of sex?" he asked her.

"Yes," she said.

"Why?"

"Because I feel a criminal lack of affection in my life."

"Your parents didn't love you enough," I said. "That's the terrible thing that happened to you."

"No, it's because of who I am," she said.

"For me, it's about power," said the man who'd told us he hid from his wife. "I feel like I'm always chasing it."

"Sex is a prison," the woman with dyed-red hair said. "But it's a prison where we can run free."

"What does having a lot of sex mean to you?" Dr. Rieux repeated to me.

"Sex is normal. It's a biological compulsion. We're made to do it. I just want to do it more than most."

Arthur laughed.

"I don't have a drinking problem," Arthur said. "I drink. I get drunk. I fall down. What's the problem?'"

The woman with dyed-red hair snickered. Helena, next to Arthur, joggled her leg up and down.

"So, I want to revisit what you said at the beginning," Dr. Rieux said. "About underlying trauma. I'm not sure it's useful to isolate events in your past and say this is where it all went wrong. Events make it easier to tell people a story of who you are, but you're made of millions of moments and they're all significant. You're just you, as you said so eloquently. Certainly, cause and effect underpin our experiences, but who are we to say which cause was the most important? The best thing we can do is just say how we feel about the causes and effects. Let's focus on your encounters. How do they make you feel?"

"OK," I said, then turned to Arthur. "That joke was funny. Probably because I drink a lot."

If Dr. Rieux was irritated, he didn't show it. He pulled out a notepad and was about to write something down, then placed it aside. I'd made it clear I didn't want to be there, like the petulant teenager who says they didn't ask to be born.

"Jesus, this guy is trying to fucking help you," the woman with dyed-red hair said to me. "Stop being such a bitch."

"Whatever," I said slowly. "My encounters are the same as yours. It's not like I'm out gathering souls. I call someone or meet a stranger at a bar. We get drunk. We go to their apartment or a place on the way if it can't wait, like with the ATM, the whole reason I'm here. Or, there's a place called the Hideaway where you can get someone to go with you. It's got blinking colored lightbulbs on the sign outside. The police are always there. No one knows they're police until they find the girl.

"You said power and affection. For me it's about possessing someone. I know that's vampiric. I don't have a terrible thing that happened, I feel like the reason I'm this way is just a gray uncertainty. Honestly, I just want to get rid of myself. Is that depression? Is that spiritual? Is that animal? Maybe sex is for me that grand symbolic performance of returning to the womb. I want to disappear inside. It's not just symbolic. But I got an ex-girlfriend pregnant once. I saw the pink liquid they sucked out of her—we couldn't even make a corpse.

"I fly people to the Hamptons. For Chariots. The luxury helicopter company. A few months ago, I took a couple to Montauk. They were so drunk they thought no one could see them, like the lights on the ground and the pilot right in front of them were images on a television. They took off their clothes. I don't think they saw me watching, or if they did, they didn't care. It was strange how separate they seemed, not to me, but to each other. It was like they were having sex with the idea of each other. They were each having sex with their own deceptions. Sex can be selfish. Sometimes sex is the loneliest thing you can do."

I realized I'd been staring at the floor the whole time, so I looked up. The woman with dyed-red hair was rubbing her hands. Her skin looked dry. Across from me, the woman with bangs flushed. She was pointing her phone toward me.

"Are you recording me?" I asked suddenly.

She looked at Dr. Rieux, then back at me.

"Yes, it's my job."

I sprang out of my seat.

"Paul, please sit," he said. "Gemma, can you shut it off?"

But I was already gone.

Outside, the police were setting up blue A-frame barricades. There was a stack in front of the brownstone. A heavy officer with a wet cough saw me struggling to get past them. He called over a few others and they dragged them away. He asked for my driver's license and wrote down my information.

"You don't live here," he observed.

"No, I've been seeing a therapist."

"For what?"

"Afraid of the dark."

"Is it helping?"

"Just got cured."

The police officer nodded and handed back my license.

"What are these barricades for?" I asked him.

"Dinner party," he grinned.

I walked toward Amsterdam. The street was lined with glossy trash bags, some gashed and leaking coffee grounds and onion skins. A younger man told me earlier in the week that the activists had made an unlikely deal with the sanitation workers. No pick-up on any block with a precinct. I could still hear the warm rasp of the man's voice in my ear. I remember the dark crimson walls of the bar, and the amateur paintings of old saints on the wall, but I don't remember what he looked like.

Across the avenue, a man who dressed as a woman and maybe was a woman pirouetted in front of an expensive Turkish restaurant. He wore a loose sun-faded tunic and, with a pair of old foam headphones clamped over his ears, wired to a Sony Walkman attached to his waist, danced in brash arcs. I felt elated to see him, or her—this person in particular. The world still held a possibility of joy, even if that joy was in spite of the world that made it.

I was about to cross when I felt a hand on my shoulder.

It was Dr. Rieux.

A red-checked scarf plunged over the collar of his unbuttoned herringbone coat.

"I'd like to talk to you," he said.

"I'm not going back."

"I know. I won't ask you to. I'd like to propose something else. Let me buy you a cup of coffee."

"Fuck off."

"Please," he said.

Against my better judgment, I followed him to a nearby café with terra cotta floors and a nearly depleted pastry case. Two women stood in line in front of us, both dressed in unnecessarily long flannel shirts that draped well over their knees. Fashion had become satire for some women—they wore leather jackets that ended a foot above their waist, or mini-sweaters with batwing sleeves, or business-like shirts with exaggerated funnel cuffs.

Dr. Rieux ordered us both an espresso and we sat down.

"Why was she recording me?" I demanded.

"That was my phone. I'm sorry, I thought I told you that I review the sessions later," he said. "Gemma just holds it for me."

"Why?"

"To find the patterns in what people are saying."

"Does everyone know?"

"It's in the pre-screening forms I make you sign. But it doesn't matter. Therapy requires trust and yours has been demolished. There's no winning it back. So I'm going to suggest something a little unorthodox. Do you have a car?"

"No."

"Good. I have a country house on the Delaware River. It's about two hours away by bus. Lots of books and a fireplace. I'd like you to stay there a while. There isn't a bar for twenty miles. But you can walk to get groceries and things. That might sound a bit drastic—to cut yourself off—but I have a strong suspicion it may help you."

"You're crazy."

"We can take it a day at a time. One day equals one session. I'll mark you down for attendance."

"You don't even know me."

"There's very little to do," he continued. "Which is the point. You can take a bus as soon as tomorrow morning. How are you on money?"

"I can't pay you."

"I mean for supplies."

"Why would you do this? I could burn your house down."

"I genuinely want to help you."

"But what if I burn down your house?"

"Then, you burn it down."

"It's not going to help."

"I've done some unusual things in my practice. Sometimes it doesn't work out, but sometimes it does. I'm just following my instinct." He paused. "What's yours telling you to do?"

Outside, a yellow cab pulled up and some activists leapt out. With heavy duffel bags they hurtled toward the police station. A woman in a lavish shearling coat took their place in the cab, tossing a cigarette onto the sidewalk through the open window. I considered this inconsequential exchange, which had taken years to manufacture—the woman and the activists had followed separate trajectories for decades, from birth to the present, oblivious to the existence of the other—and the climactic moment went unnoticed by both. All those pieces conspiring, for years, in the end, for nothing.

I took a bus from Port Authority the next morning. A young goth slept in the back next to the bathroom, which reeked of antiseptic. I've always admired goths. They really commit to the mask. The woman seated next to me watched an action movie on her phone and discreetly pumped her fist. I spent most of my time looking out the unwashed window at the gray ranks of trees. Here and there I saw a sign in support of the police. One, which was painted on the roof of a collapsing barn, read "Lick the Badge."

In Cochecton, the bus dropped me next to an antique store with a wooden canon stationed on the lawn. It had big spoked wheels and pointed at the sky. Dr. Rieux had instructed me to walk south for two miles before taking Coughlin Road, which turned into Ackerman. From there, I found the house easily, a defenseless cottage with old blue and brown apothecary bottles in the windows.

Inside, it smelled like the underside of a buried stone.

I toured the first floor—a dark country kitchen, a showerless bathroom, and a living room with worn leather chairs, a long narrow table crowded with art books, and a musty brick fireplace. Upstairs, there was a full bathroom, a library, and the bedroom.

I went down to the basement to turn on the water. Dr. Rieux had instructed me to rotate the red handle ninety-degrees counterclockwise, followed by the blue one, then to lift the valve marked "Water." The pipes rattled and groaned. I went upstairs and tried the faucet. It juddered violently but nothing came out. Then, the pipe underneath the sink cracked.

Freezing cold water sloshed everywhere onto the floor.

I threw down whatever rags and towels I could find in the kitchen, but the water came geysering out. I took off my shirt and threw it onto the floor, then ran to the basement to shut the valve. The water flowed continuously for ten minutes before slowing to a trickle.

I found more towels in the two bathrooms, plus there were a pair of closets at the top of the stairs, one with a box of videotapes, the other crammed with linens, pillows and some extra washcloths. I sopped up the water with everything I could find but not before the wooden planks started to whiten like caked milk.

I had no choice but to call Dr. Rieux.

"A pipe burst," I said. "Under the kitchen sink."

"When you turned on the water?"

"Yes. I'm sorry but it took a while to clean up. The floor turned white."

"It's an old unsealed floor. Not to worry. Frozen pipes. I'll call the plumber."

"I'm sorry. I'll take the bus back tomorrow morning."

"Actually, it'll help if you're there to let him in. He may not come for a couple of days though. Can you rough it until then?"

I didn't say anything.

"It's not your fault, Paul," he said. "Let's just stick to the terms. It's not a big deal."

He hung up.

I went outside. I followed a path that led down to the river. The sound of construction workers chopping up scaffolding, trucks backing up, sirens, buses and the constant murmur of conversations never bothered me, but the water gnashing and tumbling over the rocks did—I found it very stressful. Sometimes I hear people advocate for a grand return to nature, but this didn't feel like any homecoming. I watched a heavy branch get carried away in the current before I filled two large water bottles and returned to the house.

There wasn't any food in the refrigerator, so I walked the four miles into town. A row of houses languishing in fallen leaves led to the post office, and across the street was the general store. I roamed the aisles, collecting bread, eggs, coffee, beer, and other basics. In back, there was a glass display case full of hand-carved figurines from American history, so I bought an Amelia

Earhart, which always seemed to me like a better talisman than Icarus, the one most pilots championed.

A light snow fell as I trudged back to the house. I had the road to myself until a man stepped out of the woods. At first, I didn't see the carbon black rifle, almost organic in shape, in his gloved hands. He walked in front of me without so much as a glance, as if he were in my world but I wasn't in his. He disappeared into the trees.

Back at the cottage, I made an omelet on a cast iron pan and drank two beers. The sky darkened into a heavy bruise. In the library upstairs, I pulled down *Great Expectations* and read the first hundred pages, then drank a third beer in the bedroom, trying to watch TV but there wasn't any cable, just an old VCR.

I grew restless. I wanted to go out and find someone. I wanted to persuade them to come with me to a dark place. I wanted to feel their warm skin underneath their shirt. I wanted to smell them. I wanted to search for their open mouth in the dark. I wanted them to sense my longing. I wanted to feel their longing against me. I wanted to reach inside them. I wanted to make them tremble. I wanted to tremble too.

That night I dreamed about my mother. She was lying on the street in another woman's body, then rose into her own. Her eyes and lips were smeared. A torn metallic dress hung off her shoulder and her black hair was like two chaotic trapezoids. We walked in darkness to the edge of a lake, and she undressed in front of me. I was young when she died, but I'd seen her body many times, and she looked the same as then, abrupt and insinuating. Like a child I focused on her hard nipples. Then, without a word, she dove into the lake and the water made a halo where she entered.

The next morning, after coffee and another hundred pages of *Great Expectations*, I went upstairs to change. I paused in front of the closets, remembering the one with the videotapes. There were dozens of them heaped in a large cardboard box. The snout of an old VHS camera poked through the pile. Each cassette had been marked with a date by the same hand, the most recent from last year.

I went into the bedroom and put in one of the tapes.

Arthur and Helena came onto the screen.

They were having sex on the bed where I now sat, their bodies shimmering with video grain. At Arthur's urging, Helena flattened underneath him. He crawled backward athletically, shoved her legs apart and bowed his head. It grew quiet in the room. Her arm slid across the sheet. Her breathing changed and she stared up at the ceiling. Then, strangely, she turned to the camera and simpered. I didn't understand why. It was a lurid grin that lasted for an uncomfortable minute. Then, she scissored her legs and rolled Arthur onto his back. She rose and straddled him. I could see only the crown of his head and the bridge of his nose. He reached for her back. Helena moaned. She began to sway, then pitched forward. She cried out when she came.

Arthur slid away and left the frame. He returned a few moments later with two cloth strips, which he used to bind Helena's wrists to the bedposts. Helena, supine, looked at him without kindness or contempt. He climbed onto her, so they were face to face, reached between his legs to arrange himself and staggered forward, straightening his arms to steady himself. His backbone jutted out like a snake's skeleton half-buried in sand. I'd lost sight of Helena except for her legs, which curled in the air.

After he finished, I took out the tape, then fed another into the slot.

Arthur kneeled on the bed, facing the camera. He had a long scar across his shoulder, which I hadn't noticed in the first video. Helena came over to him in just gray jersey underwear, her hair blending into the dark wall. She coiled around him. He closed his eyes. Again, she turned to the camera in the strangest way, sarcastic, overconfident. I wondered who she was performing for.

Had they filmed themselves for Dr. Rieux? Was making sex tapes part of their therapy? Did Dr. Rieux want me to find these tapes? How could that possibly help me? Or was this actually Arthur and Helena's house? Why would he send me there? Was she performing for Arthur, or herself, or a stranger? Did it turn them on while they were filming or later when they watched?

I played more videos—it was always just the two of them on the same bed—until I heard a loud knock on the door.

I shut off the TV and went downstairs. A man with a copper-colored beard and no moustache stood outside holding a red Milwaukee bag.

"Plumber," he said.

"Oh, right. Come in."

I let him inside. He whistled when he saw the kitchen floor.

"Outstanding," he said. "That's outstanding work."

Without another word, he vanished under the sink. I stood by the refrigerator and watched his legs kick around violently. It seemed like maybe he was getting strangled under there.

"Hand me the P-trap from the front pocket of the bag, would you?" he said. "The curvy one."

He worked for several minutes, then asked me to go downstairs and turn on the water. When I returned, he was standing in the kitchen with a look of triumph, as if he'd just let out a silent fart. He turned on the sink to show me it was working now.

"That wood is gonna need to come out," he said, gesturing at the floor.

"I'll tell him," I said.

He looked confused for a moment, then walked to the door. Before leaving, he turned and asked, "Do you hunt?"

"No."

"Fish?"

"No."

"Drink?"

"Yes."

He nodded, then left.

I went back upstairs to watch more tapes.

More and more I fixated on Helena. She behaved so erratically, undercutting pleasure with her ironic mask. Maybe the camera was to blame, but then why set it up? Was Arthur aware? He seemed dedicated to his own resolution that I thought not. Again and again, she turned and vamped in the most self-conscious way, revealing what I took to be a painful insecurity. She seemed very alone, and even a little pathetic.

After a long while, I got sick of watching. It'd gotten dark out. I felt empty after doing nothing else all day. I turned over one of the VHS tapes in my hands. Dr. Rieux, and maybe Arthur and Helena, had been playing some kind of game with me. I didn't get the point, but it didn't matter, I didn't want to play it. I decided to leave the next morning. I'd take the next bus back to New York.

In my wallet I carry a picture of my mother. The photograph is at least twenty-five years old. The color has faded. She has on a long jacket and is standing against a white marble wall with her hair rough and dark and black circles under her eyes, and she's smiling in a what else can go wrong kind of way.

In the morning, I went outside. A thin layer of new snow covered the ground like sugar. I hiked down to the river. A string of Canadian geese flew over the split between the trees. I could barely hear them. They were tough birds, tougher than they looked. Most pilots hate them because they got pulled into their engines.

When I returned to the house, there was a red hatchback pulling onto the side of the road. I thought the plumber had returned, or maybe a contractor had come to rip up the floor.

But it was Helena.

She got out of the car, holding a large cup of coffee.

"Hello," she waved.

I nodded and went inside the house. She came in after me and immediately seized the copy of *Great Expectations* I'd left on the table.

"Do you like it?" she asked.

"I read it in high school," I said. "I couldn't remember why Miss Havisham caught on fire."

"A barrel of laughs, you might say."

"Have you read it?"

"'From the agony of his disenchantment comes a work of heartbreaking genius,'" she read from the back cover. "Not my cup of tea. I don't read much, actually. I think movies are better for learning about the human condition."

I'd never heard someone say that phrase aloud—the human condition. I thought maybe she was making fun of me.

"Is this your house?" I asked.

She stretched for her toes and exhaled loudly.

"You really did a number on this floor," she said.

"Is this your house?" I asked again.

"No," she said, returning her attention to the book. "Why would you ask that?"

"Because you're here in the kitchen."

Maybe human condition was a normal thing to say.

I went to the stove and put on the kettle.

"So, besides the agony of your disenchantment and destroying the floor, what have you been doing?"

"Do you have a message for me or something?"

"I just come here sometimes."

"But it's not your house," I said.

"Dr. Rieux let us stay here the last time we were in therapy. About a year ago."

"So it didn't work."

"Arthur and I used to come here when we had one kind of issue. Now, we have another kind of issue. He's only into men now. He thinks Dr. Rieux can talk him out of it."

"I assumed if you're a sex addict, you'd be open to anything."

"Well, we're not all desperate."

It was strange to be insulted by someone who you've watched having sex on television.

"Did you know I'd be here?"

"I came to get something."

"If you want, you can have the place. I'm going to pack and get the next bus."

"Alright," she said. "Whatever."

She waited a while before following me up to the bedroom. The tapes were still scattered on the floor. I didn't say anything. Neither did she. She just stood in the doorway, watching me shove underwear into my duffel bag. She came over when I sat down on the edge of the bed. Helena arched her eyebrows in an exaggerated manner. I leaned in to make the expression go away.

We kissed for a while. I felt like I was falling. She dragged my hand to her legs and started moving against my palm. With my other hand I braced myself as we listed onto the bed. I unbuttoned her shirt, then took off her bra. She was younger than me, athletic, with boyish shoulders and dark moles down her neck and chest. The sunlight made a rectangle on the bed next to us. When I crawled onto her, the light slid over us like a sheet. We moved together for a while. We looked into each other's eyes when we came.

In that moment, I'm embarrassed to admit, I wanted to make her pregnant.

I don't think I can explain that. When I try to unravel the web of invisible threads that make me do what I do and want what I want, I only get glimpses of pictures and dreams. It's just that it felt inevitable, more like a memory than fantasy. I had to have her. I wanted it to live beyond the ash.

For some time, I watched her breath go in and out. Her skin felt warm against mine. Around the bed were all the tapes she'd made with Arthur like a lair of bones. A strong wind flicked the tree branches against the outside of the cottage. I thought of the plume of smoke that surrounded my mother in her dream.

Helena lifted the sheet over us and crawled onto me.

After a while, we started again.

In the afternoon, I got the cardboard box and we packed the tapes. We didn't talk about them. I carried the box to the hatchback and placed them inside, then returned to the kitchen to make sandwiches. We ate them at the table and drank the remaining beers. Afterward, we went down to the river and ran our hands through the cold water.

We left after dark. There weren't many cars on the road. Helena talked about Arthur. She said she had money and someone to stay with. She then told me a long story about a friend of hers who got into some trouble and had to stay at a clinic, and how she pretended to be a doctor to get him released. She made it sound like a completely natural thing to do.

From the highway I could see Yonkers glowing. It took me a while to realize it was on fire. It was the same in Riverdale and Washington Heights. We passed several burning buildings. The police had been preparing. Helena raced down the West Side Highway. I lived near Morningside Park but instead of taking the exit, she drove all the way to the Boat Basin and turned onto 79th Street, chattering the whole time to turn around but never listening.

Fire trucks staggered through traffic. Sirens pierced us from every direction. People ran through shadows. We inched up Amsterdam, trying to make sense of the chaos. When we crossed 82nd, I saw the police station near Columbus burning. From what I could tell, there was a fire every ten or twelve blocks.

They hit all the precincts, I said.

Helena gripped the wheel with white fingers. It was impossible to turn around. I said we should go to my apartment.

A platoon of bicyclers dressed in black streamed onto the avenue, maneuvering through cars and using hand signals to communicate. They wore masks so we couldn't see their faces. Some took to the sidewalk, followed by other activists on foot. On 100th Street between Amsterdam and Columbus, they gathered next to a row of police cars rinsed in flames.

As we approached St. John the Divine, people ran downstream. Not activists. Some of them were cradling exotic animals in their arms. At first, I thought they were people fleeing with their pets. But I saw a woman with an armadillo and another with a limp fox. A man dragged a llama onto the sidewalk, which wrenched away from him and ran. It was the Blessing of the Animals. The cathedral was on fire too.

Helena pulled over. There was nowhere to go.

"I can't do this," she said.

She was shaking.

I saw an animal walking in circles on the sidewalk. I thought it was a rat but it was too big and round and it had a white face. Its eyes glowed like haunted glass. I jumped out of the car. Helena yelled but I went anyway. It was an opossum, badly burned. Its fur was covered in what looked like thick grease and its long tail was raw and bleeding. I heard Helena calling to me from the car but I didn't respond. I took off my shirt and gently wrapped it around the opossum, then carried it back to the car.

"If it dies, we can bury it," I said.

The Lamp

She cleared off the table except for the lamp, a gift from her husband. A mosaic of sea glass glued onto a post of Lucite, cloaked in an off-white lampshade. She wondered which was worse, being a creative person with no taste or a convenience store of resentment. While dusting the table with a rag, she saw that the lampshade had been singed on the back—where the light had touched the fabric, an amber blister. She had neither the heart to throw it away nor the stomach to keep it. She had nothing inside her at all anymore. That had been her gift to him.

Break Glass in Case of Simulacrum

Until last summer, my life had seemed routine. I lived in a northern suburb of Philadelphia with my wife, Jamie, and our three unexceptional boys, Finnegan, Chase, and Niles. Every day I read the newspaper on the commuter train to Penn Center and then walked two blocks to Lombard International, where I worked as an attorney. At five, I returned home, ate an unsurprising dinner with my family, and wrestled the boys to bed.

Seasons passed. I drove by green fields and watched them gray, I drove by gray fields and watched them green. Crows' feet forked behind Jamie's eyes. The boys became less likely to get run over by a car and more likely to die from an overdose. Of course I worried but it was accompanied by a fatalistic detachment, as if we were all just passengers in each other's dreams.

Then, one night, everything changed. I won't call it an accident because it may have been intentional, it's impossible to know. It's like asking why God created suffering—no matter your answer, there isn't any certainty. I was coming home on the commuter train, and we were racing between stations, dropping off passengers and closing all the loops we'd started that morning, and as we neared King of Prussia, the overhead lights began to flicker. Suddenly, the whole train—the walls, the seats, even the passengers— shattered into ash.

The next moment, I was seated at the dinner table with my family, and I couldn't account for how I got there. It felt like I'd been pulled from a deep sleep and whatever dream I was having had been scrubbed away. Chase and Jamie were at my left, Finnegan at my right. Niles sat across from me, stabbing a piece of chicken with a fork. I saw that his nose was bleeding, so I rushed to his side, and as I soaked up the blood with a napkin, I looked into his drowned eye and saw a stranger reflected there.

Not a stranger, exactly. It was more like an idea of a person.

Like code.

That's when I remembered the train.

By all accounts I should've been dead, yet somehow I'd been rescued, and then dropped into my home. I don't know why but right away I decided not to tell Jamie. I wanted to keep it to myself. To be honest, I'm not sure how I held it together. I should've ran into the street and stepped in front of a bus. Instead, I felt euphoric. I knew a secret, maybe the only secret in the world worth knowing. Over the next few days, I went about my routine as if nothing had happened. But all the while, on the train, at the office, at home, I looked for clues.

I found signs everywhere, and it was almost comical that I hadn't noticed them before. After work, on my way to Penn Center, I stopped to watch a cocker spaniel panting in the shade. It looked just like the one from my neighborhood. The two of them had the exact same chocolate chip pattern, and their barks, rasping to the point of sickly, were also identical. They even wore the same green grosgrain collar.

Soon I awoke to other replicas in the city. At first it was just dogs. But then, as I explored surrounding neighborhoods, I saw people repeating like background characters in a video game.

I suspected they were clones.

A week later, another breakthrough. I was sitting on a park bench and began to document the shapes of clouds. After paying just the slightest bit of attention, I discovered there were only twelve unique forms. Although they broke apart or joined together, they were always migrating to or from a core shape. For two more days I tracked them, and I found that the clouds traveled in only three directions, separated by exactly 120 degrees, and they moved at only one speed—80 mph.

The geometry was so pristine. The clouds couldn't be real. They were programs. And if the clouds weren't real, then the replicas weren't clones. They were surely programs too.

I could see, hear, touch, taste, and smell. I had emotions. I had the power to reason. I had a wife and three kids. I had a lucrative career. I had a favorite meal (steak frites), a favorite color (green), a favorite hockey player

(Eric Desjardins), a favorite band (Dire Straits), a favorite toothpaste brand (Crest), and a favorite memory (when my mother let me sit in the front seat of her station wagon during a drive-through car wash).

Was all the data programmed? Was anything mine?

Remembering the reflection in my son's eye, I questioned whether I was even alive, if anyone was, Jamie, my sons, who were the gods of this nervous breakdown, what was the purpose of the simulation, was I the only subject?

That night, I cornered Jamie in our bedroom.

"What is it?" she asked, folding her arms. Outside, a heavy summer rain beat against the air conditioner. Jamie had asked me many times to drape a towel over the AC to mute the sound of the rain, but I'd put it off. I could sense that she was listening to the loud drumming sound and calculating how badly she'd sleep that night.

"Something terrible has happened," I blurted out, unsure how to proceed.

"What is it? Work?" she panicked.

"No, nothing like that."

I took a deep breath.

"Have you ever noticed that the clouds move in only three directions?" I asked, trying to sound scientific.

Her eyes flickered with surprise, then annoyance.

"Clouds?" she asked.

"Yes," I said.

"Are you being serious?"

"Have you seen anything like that? Something that should be very complicated physically, but isn't?"

"I can think of simple things that turn out to be shockingly complicated," she said.

We'd met at Lombard International. We were both assigned to the Bergman account, which required many NDAs and late nights eating takeout and drinking Sauvignon Blanc. We bonded over our mutual hatred of Chardonnays as well as Bergman—the man had illegally funneled hundreds of thousands of dollars into a shell company in Panama, and it was our job to scrape what we could after the government froze his assets. Bergman was a scumbag, but he was also a guy you could build a career on, and apparently a marriage.

Our wedding was objectively extravagant, the kind of event you would expect from people like us, anodyne people with money, people who visited a battleship on a Saturday afternoon for fun. When Finnegan came along, Jamie quit Lombard to stay with him. Then, Chase and Niles arrived, and we were permanently chiseled into our roles. It never occurred to me to want something I couldn't get from my commute.

When we fell in love, I would've slit my own throat for Jamie. Then she raised our boys. She made me write my father's eulogy after he died. She cheered for the Flyers even though she hated hockey. When she found a mouse in the bread drawer, she ruthlessly flushed it down the toilet. We had just enough sex. Our love deepened like a book read many times.

How could someone be imaginary if you can't imagine life without them?

It wasn't the rain that kept us up that night, it was the heat. It hung in the air like an insoluble shame. Each day had been muggier than the last, and the AC offered little relief. It was like a virus we had to sweat out. Jamie had no idea what I was talking about with the clouds, and I began to doubt what I'd seen and experienced. I questioned whether I was the one unraveling. I decided to do something drastic, although not without precedent.

The next day, I woke Finnegan early and left the others a note: *Going on a hike. Back at 2.* Fog congested the surrounding woods as we drove north on highway 476, but the sun burned it off by the time we turned east onto the 22. The whole time, I let Finnegan fuss with the radio stations. He had terrible taste in music but I wanted him to be happy. Mount Minsi wasn't far.

Shortly after Allentown, though, Finnegan said he needed to use the bathroom. I took the next exit—it was the only reason we got off the highway, we would've kept going otherwise. The country road was wall to wall trees, there were no restaurants or gas stations, and after a couple of miles I was about to switch directions when we came over a hill and saw a windowless building ahead. On the front, in red letters, next to the same fighting lion crest my company used, it said "Lombard Research Center."

I banked on the side of the road.

It's hard to explain my state of mind in that moment. Here I was, on the way to Mt. Minsi, with Finnegan, who I planned to sacrifice, or at least I was pretending that I would—I'd convinced myself the programmers would swoop in and rescue him like a satisfied God, or if they didn't, he'd bleed green numbers, he wouldn't actually die—but right when we're passing the only exit that could possibly lead to this mysterious Lombard building, Finnegan asks to use the bathroom. It was too coincidental to be a coincidence.

"You want me to go in the woods?" he asked.

"No, don't get out of the car."

"OK," he said nervously.

I scanned the parking lot for life. The few cars there gleamed like mirrors in the scalding light of the sun.

"Lombard," I murmured.

"Dad?"

"Yeah."

"Can we find a bathroom?"

After Finnegan relieved himself at a heavily air-conditioned Burger King a few miles away, we returned home.

"What happened to the hike?" Jamie asked at the door. She smelled like coffee and just brushed teeth. Her damp shirt clung to her skin.

"Finnegan," I said, rolling my eyes.

I snuck my laptop into the bathroom and entered "Lombard Bethlehem" into the search bar. There were numerous mentions of Dr. Johannes Lombard, an orthopedic surgeon in South Africa, but I also saw a Glass Door page of employee reviews for a company called Auperion. Most were written by programmers with familiar complaints—long hours, inadequate equipment, lack of recognition—but one of the reviews stuck out. It'd been left by "anonymous," and it said, "Descartes would be so proud of us."

I typed in Auperion.com but the site appeared to be down. There were navigation tabs for Mission Statement, Research, Education, Calendar, Staff, and Contact Us, but the only ones that worked were Calendar, which had no listed events, and Staff, a grid of several employee photographs.

As I scrolled down, I came across a photograph of a woman in the fifth or sixth row. It's hard to explain the way she looked to me, or maybe it's the way I looked at her, I don't know the difference now—it was like a hand reached through my chest and squeezed, as if my heart were a rat, and the hand were squeezing all the life from it, and no matter how much it scratched, the rat would never escape, the hand had a permanent death grip on it, unclenching only when it was about to die, so it could get a breath, and then the hand would clench again, so my rat heart was trapped in a state of perpetual thrashing, it would never be free and it could never die.

The woman was beautiful, but not in an embarrassing way. She was beautiful but also plain, the way the sun is beautiful and plain, the way golden hour is just plain sunlight. Dark lashes crowned her round, amused eyes, and she had a wide, unbalanced smile, as if she knew a secret, some wry joke that made her laugh. Brown hair fell in waves across her shoulders, and she seemed young, perhaps very young, still rooted to the myth of her own possibility.

It was just a photograph, and yet I felt the awful terror and violence of love wash over me like a tsunami crashing against a clapboard shack, its slats and panels shattering under the water, pulverized into smithereens and swept away, so pathetically erased that you question if the shack was ever really there. I wanted to shut the laptop but I really couldn't move, and when I finally did, it was too late.

Her name was Ava Betts, or that's what it said underneath the photograph. Immediately I searched her name but was overwhelmed with imposters. There were hundreds of links to social media profiles, marked-safe lists, high school track times, news articles, intramural rosters, blogs, obituaries, census reports, and comments. I hunted through them all, finding no one.

Jamie gave me a dark look when I came out. I held the laptop close to my chest as if it were a machine cleaning out my blood. She stood in the middle of the hallway, blocking my path. I thought of Ava's photograph and my heart juddered, discomfited by my wife's stance.

"Finnegan told me what happened."

I nodded like a criminal.

"Can you talk to me?" she asked, and then answered, with insistence,

"You *can* talk to me."

"I tried," I said.

"Keep trying," she said.

"OK," I said. "I'll try."

On Monday morning, I left for work at the normal hour. But instead of going to the office, I called in sick and returned to Bethlehem. I parked close to the door so I could see everyone but far enough away to avoid scrutiny. Sweat trickled down my cheeks like tears. The air outside was disgusting, it carried with it the smell of rotting plants. In only a couple of months the leaves would crisp, and the trees would gray and shudder, but it was hard to imagine anything ever changing, the thermometer was stuck at 98.6 degrees.

I think by then I knew what I was. Unconsciously, I'd figured it out, even if I had yet to articulate it—that I had no body, no *real* body, anyway, my body was just a performance, and my real self was being kept alive. The anonymous review, my video game–like world, the Lombard building, Ava's photograph—especially Ava's photograph—all got me there. Were Jamie and the boys real, or were they software—in my heart, a heart I didn't really have, I think I knew the answer to that too.

Yet I was certain that Ava was real. She was unlike anyone or anything I'd ever seen. Wouldn't I know the difference between a person and a god? The other Lombard staffers looked like placeholders, like avatars, but Ava had pierced me. The idea that I'd fallen in love with her was as insane as it was inexorable. There I was, mired in a swamp of desperate longing. My brain had become a moth.

People left the building between 12 and 1. Many ate their lunch alone in the privacy of their cars. Some napped. A short round man vaped near the bike rack. I didn't see Ava. I wondered what she sounded like. With only the one photograph, I had to fill in blanks. I imagined her voice clear and unvarnished, but that her words came out clenched, like she grinded the edges of them in her teeth, and it made me think she'd endured some cruelty in life, what had she staggered through already.

I imagined she smelled like a beautiful absence, like the clean cold smell of winter.

I sat there for hours watching the front door. I barely moved, visualizing her walking out and her round eyes lighting up with recognition when she saw me from afar. I imagined getting out of the car and nervously approaching. I imagined taking her hand and feeling the incontestable warmth of her skin. I imagined her agonizing lips and my stomach hollowing out in the terror of a first kiss and the terror of every kiss after that, each one more ruinous. I imagined kneeling in front of her and taking down her jeans. I imagined pressing my mouth between her legs. I imagined her body as if it were a grave.

Everything I imagined.

As the workers returned to their cars at the end of the day, a feeling of dread welled inside me, and then relief, and then back to dread, the most horrible dread, that I'd never see her, at the Lombard parking lot or anywhere, because I wanted Ava, I needed her, already I was coming apart without her, and I was going to be trapped alone in this room without walls and forever consumed by this pitiless and painful desire.

I returned home for dinner. The boys tore into their food like soldiers. I had no appetite. What was the point of food? Jamie talked about a funny thing that happened at the town dump but I hardly listened. Instead, I wondered why they didn't write eating out of our scripts. After all, we didn't need it. Was hunger a button they pressed, or did I really feel it, what was and was not a hoax? Again I thought of Ava, and how she might look when slurping noodles from a bowl of ramen—humiliated or nonchalant? Was she effective at holding chopsticks? How did she drink a beer?

I called in sick for the rest of the week. Every morning, I drove back to the building in Bethlehem. Each day, I parked closer to the front. On Friday, I rolled down the window and laid my arm upon the ledge. It felt like a transgression, a part of my body protruding from the car like that. The metal was blistering. All the while, I sat listlessly in the driver's seat, exhausted from the heat, exhausted from thinking about Ava.

That night, after dinner, Jamie put the boys to bed, and I sat on the couch checking email. As I was finishing up, a new message appeared at the top of my inbox, from abetts@lombard.com. There was no subject line. I pushed the laptop away, crippled with hope. Jamie was upstairs bargaining with the boys to brush their teeth. I had a small window to myself.

Gutless, I opened it.

There were no words in the body. Only a Webex link. I used Webex at work for video conferences. My hands began to tremble. The full corruption of my longing flamed in my blood. I was going to see her. I was going to hear her. I'd shot an arrow across the river and held it as it traveled and was standing on the other side.

Ava.

I clicked the link.

When the video came online, I saw three men gawking at me from inside some kind of laboratory. One of them had a beard, and they wore long white lab coats.

"Hey!" the one on the right called out excitedly. "Can you see us?"

"Yes," I said. "Yes, I can see you."

Slowly the room came into focus. Several laptops were scattered on tables. Shelves were cluttered with books and beakers and there were four monitors hanging on the far wall. On a metal examination table, I saw a large glass cylinder hooked up to hoses and wires that fed into computer equipment and a large red oxygen tank. And inside the cylinder was a human brain, speared with cannulae, floating in what looked like dishwater.

"It's like seeing yourself in a mirror, right?" the man laughed.

The brain looked like a congealed fetus. There were short, shallow trenches all over, meandering paths that led nowhere. It was impossible to believe it, that everything I'd ever experienced, that I was experiencing in that very moment, was occurring inside that furrowed mass, and that it contained an entire universe of extravagant cities and stars and sorrows and ordinary laughter, and I'd never really gone anywhere, I'd never really loved anyone, all I'd ever done was pretend.

The man with the beard hopped onto the table. He unbuckled his pants and began to urinate into the vat. The other men cheered. Their faces were familiar, I'd seen them at the Lombard building, they had avatars in the simulation, my world was a simulacrum. When the bearded man finished urinating, he turned and squatted over the vat with his pants around his ankles, positioning himself to defecate.

But one of the other men interrupted him with a baseball bat, slamming it against the table right at the foot of the cylinder. The bearded man hopped off laughing.

"No!" I screamed. "Please!"

The other man lifted the bat again. I was about to watch my own murder. I was living in and seeing the movie of my death being filmed in one world and projected in another. Kill the head and the body will die. The man reached back further, his eyes lustrous. I braced for the end as he slammed the bat down, just missing me by an inch.

"Strike two!" he screamed.

The third man approached the vat. He climbed onto the table with his back to the camera, and when he turned, I saw that he was cradling an erection.

"Stop!" I begged.

"What are you doing?" Jamie barked from the stairwell.

Instinctively I slapped the laptop shut and looked at her in despair. I wanted to tell her that I was about to be murdered, that our whole world was about to shatter. I searched her eyes for understanding, knowing the bat could come down at any moment, and then suddenly I felt a rush of endorphins flood my body, all of them tied to shame, not nothingness.

"You're screaming and you're sweating like a psychopath. Are you doing some kind of interactive snuff porn thing? What the fuck is wrong with you?"

She marched upstairs. I didn't know what she'd seen. I didn't know what I'd seen either. Maybe they hadn't killed me because I'd shut the laptop. Maybe Jamie had saved my life. Maybe they'd programmed her to come and interrupt me at that exact moment, the way they'd programmed Finnegan's bladder on the highway.

I went to the car and sat for a while, debating what had happened and whether to drive to Bethlehem—the Lombard building was my only connection, but I'd never seen Ava there—when my phone chimed. Another email had come in, again from abetts@lombard.com, with the subject line: "Open now." Again I clicked a WebEx link in the body of the email. I didn't want to, but what choice did I have?

Instead of a laboratory, I was looking at an empty highway through the windshield of a car. The camera must've been propped up on the dashboard. There was no sound. It was daytime—the sky was sheeted with clouds, and trees lined both sides of the road. I saw a sign for Harleysville before the car turned off the highway. Then, I saw a field I recognized next to a Holiday Inn. The car pulled into the hotel parking lot. It was in Kulpsville, just a few towns away.

I began to drive, my phone face-up on the passenger seat so I could continue to watch. The driver or one of the unseen passengers turned the camera around so that it faced the back seat. I couldn't see anyone, I still couldn't hear any sound, but there I was, stuffed inside a cardboard box, with medical equipment heaped all around me.

Nothing happened for a while. The camera remained focused on the brain. That allowed me to make up some time. I raced to the hotel as fast as I could. I thought I could save myself from whatever the technicians were planning to do. Drop me off the roof, maybe. When I was about ten miles away, the box and all the medical equipment were dragged from the back seat. Then someone grabbed the camera and the screen went dark.

I'd just parked in the lot when the picture reappeared. The camera was pointed at a room number, 3H, and the door opened. Shortly after, the camera was propped against the television so that it framed the entirety of the bed. I trampled up the stairs to the third floor and ran down the hall to 3H. The door was unlocked.

I entered just as Ava walked into frame. She cradled the vat carefully and laid it down to rest on a ramp of pillows. Several hoses and wires spilled over the side of the bed, and Ava climbed onto the other side, lying down across from the vat, and I followed her onto the bed, lying where the vat was, where I was, across from her, from across a world that didn't exist except inside the brain she was lying across from.

She was exactly as I imagined, her brown hair soft against her shoulders, her cheeks like cherries, a lightly mocking smile, her round eyes full of innocence and catastrophe. There was no way to touch, I could only watch, a lurker of myself, overwhelmed with ecstasy and violent terror. Ava, for her part, remained very still. She seemed to be looking through the phone with a sad curiosity.

After a few minutes, she rose from the bed and walked out of the frame. I thought she'd gone to use the bathroom, and I waited for her to return, breathless and afraid, but she didn't come back, she was never going to return, I realized, she'd done what she came to do, this act of kindness, this act of cruelty. I watched the light growing dim in her world, and in mine the morning sun was brightening the room. I'd been alone for so long, alone in a world that didn't exist, and alone in a world I didn't know existed, and the two worlds had merged, I was finally completely alone for the first time.

This Is the Future Liberals Want

$\mathbf{A}$ few years ago, around the time my friends began to desert the city, to start their small, expensive restaurants in NPR towns along the eastern seaboard, or, under the pretense of really giving it a go in some affordable wastebasket like North Adams, to paint or to write, that's when I began to ride the crowded commuter trains at the end of the day, away from Grand Central, with cars full of strangers longing to get home. Those of us too late or unlucky to get a seat simmered in mutual inconvenience, jostling with one another for space as the train sped north and into Scarsdale, where we evicted enough passengers and it became easier to breathe, think, or idle near a window. Often I'd press my face against the scratched-up glass and look out at the blackened trees, the thick beastlike voids coated in textures of ivy and shadow, and I'd feel a moment of grace before the silhouettes were corrupted by the lights inside the train reflecting in the glass, illuminating the woolen seats, the conductor soldiering through the aisle in his embarrassing uniform, young women in black leather jackets scrolling their phones, bankers drinking beer, and me, a melancholic robot, separate from them and their obtainment of capital and their exhaustion and implacable feelings. Within a few hours, we'd reach the end of the line, where I'd exit the train and then reboard, so I could return home to my apartment and recharge.

My apartment building was about forty blocks to the south of Grand Central, and as I walked home that night, a parade of fire trucks and ambulances passed me on the avenue, blaring their horns and smearing red and blue light in a routine festival of emergency. I'd been thinking about the woman I'd met earlier, remembering her clothes crisp and plain like expensive paper, and her uncomplicated smile as she led me from the train, and the heavy tires of her SUV crunching over the stones of her driveway like small animal bones—I skipped down the avenue in a pitiful reverie, and

I didn't snap out of it until I arrived at the corner of my block, where the air was tipped with the acrid smell of smoke, and as I rounded the corner, I could see an orange blaze seething inside my apartment building. The windows of the cars parked along the street reflected the flames like televisions all tuned to the same disaster. Solemn men in heavy dark coats trudged between the building and the fire trucks, as if in service to ambivalence, while neighbors watched the spectacle with lurid satisfaction. No one spoke. It looked like a very powerful fire. I guessed that it'd burn all night. I had nothing to save inside, and I didn't know anyone in my building—everything we'd had in common was now incinerated and there seemed little point in striking up a conversation.

The city always took me in with the kindness of a drunk. I wandered the streets, searching the guttered eyes of strangers. Very few met my gaze and the ones who did were mad. Behind me a hunchback dragged a duffel bag overflowing with beer and soda cans. I could hear it scuffing against the cement, for six or seven blocks he followed me until he found a garbage can to argue with. Later, a man stopped me while I was crossing Bowery. He wanted to know which way was north. I rushed him to the safety of the sidewalk and pointed at the faraway Chrysler Building, but then he followed me as I walked west, repeating in a hoarse voice, "You seem like a nice guy." I passed the Win Restaurant Supply store on Lafayette and meandered to Washington Square Park, which was deserted—the fountain, the unwashed chess tables, the arc had all been abandoned. I felt as if I were walking several feet behind myself, trying to catch the leash that led me, but it was useless, I wasn't equipped to process anything, only to feel it, and anyway the expensive apartment buildings, with gloomy doormen spying through intricate iron filigree gates, and the stony churches shrouded in dark purple shadows, and clothing shops closed for the night, and the depressing empty diners, everything was an arrow in a flow chart nudging me back to Grand Central.

It was still very early in the morning when I entered the station. The first commuter trains were just waking and wouldn't arrive until before dawn. I looked up at the magnificent ceiling, the grand drama of the constellations fixed in sea foam, and I admired the gods and the vast network of threads hidden behind them, the unseen wires in service to their stories of passion and revenge. My thoughts returned to the woman who'd brought me home earlier that night, and I thought also of my friends who'd abandoned the city, I still called them friends, the ones who'd left me behind, and I felt a pang of longing for them, and for the woman too. I decided to wait for her, though I expect that's why I'd come back in the first place, to try and make a friend of her, although she'd made it clear enough what she wanted and, by zipping me back to the train station so quickly afterwards, what she didn't. On the Arrivals monitor, the first train from Goldens Bridge wasn't due for a couple hours, so I chose to kill time by walking around the perimeter of the station like the second hand of a watch, which I found amusing, though maybe it was a joke only a machine would understand.

After several laps I drew the attention of a man in a beige trench. I noticed him noticing me—I wouldn't have otherwise. He was tall with round glasses and black hair flattened on top like a cake, and he leaned against the information booth at the center of the station, chewing on a toothpick. I felt the weight of his stare as I traveled around the perimeter. I rounded the station dozens of times until he peeled himself off and walked to the passageway that led to the Times Square shuttle, his dress shoes clacking against the pink marble floor. Of course I followed him, I had to follow him, and as I turned the corner of the passageway, his hand reached out from the shadows and pulled me into the dark.

I stumbled, reaching for something to brace my fall. My arm crashed into the wall of the man's chest. I'd been dragged behind an orange crane that was half hidden inside the entrance to a gate, and though the lights were rough I could see the man's face, his doleful eyes full of fear. I felt his hands trembling on my wrist as he searched for my pulse. The front flaps of his trench draped over my shoulders as I knelt before him. I took him into the shallow of my mouth and his breath tightened, but the sound of his moan barely registered over the ambient hum of the underground machines. I brought him in deeper, sliding him out of my mouth and then back in, and out again, and in, moving steadily until I found the disciplined rhythm of a slow-moving piston, and gently he began to knock at the back of my throat. I felt him swaying, tipping dangerously to the side, and his fingers scrunched and pulled on my hair, which steadied him. He burrowed deeper, knocking harder, but no one would come to the door, and he pounded against the futility of it, for a god to hear his knock, that's when he began to throb, that's when he swelled, spasmed, and burst like a star.

Panting, he pulled me against the crane. He looked like a spared sacrifice, surprised to still be alive.

He handed me a weathered package of tissues from his pocket. The word Kleenex was barely legible, as if the letters had been traced in the air during a snowstorm. After buttoning his trench, he returned to the passageway, and when I got back to the main part of the station, there he was again, leaned against the information booth chewing on a toothpick. It was like someone had reset the video game. Instead of walking around the perimeter, I sat down on a marble stairwell, and I watched the man survey the night's remaining fugitives and the maintenance workers hauling receptacles across the station. He saw me too, of course, but he didn't look at me in any particular way, I'd been reduced to the color of the wall or the number of a gate. I thought about approaching him, to become friends, but the first train arrived and commuters began streaming into the station, they rushed to the escalators and the exits to the streets, and more trains followed, and soon the floor was packed with an undiminished crowd of physician assistants and millionaires and other suburbanites dressed in dark wool coats, all of them afflicted by their common faith in merit. They moved in replicating swarms—it seemed as if no one left the building, people exited on one side and returned from the other, and every ten seconds a new one joined. I tried to squeeze through— the train from Goldens Bridge was imminent, surely—but someone shoved me toward the information booth. The man in the trench had fled, but I saw his pile of discarded toothpicks. I crouched down and put them in my pocket. When I stood up, several men in puffer vests had filled the space around me, their arms stiff by their sides, and behind them a phalanx of women, noses in their phones, straggled past. I thought I heard someone chanting, or maybe it was a few, I couldn't make out what they were saying, and then it seemed as if the men in vests had formed a circle around me, and there were other circles forming near us, and the circles seemed to be spinning against each other like the vertiginous gears of a watch. Like birds, people began to call out. The calls became contagious. The circle closest to me erupted into handclaps, as if a waiter had just spilled a tray of drinks onto the floor. It was a flash mob, maybe, or not, I was confused, and I shoved my way through the crowd and onto 42nd Street, underneath the Glory of Commerce, the crown on the gilded Cyclops-eye clock.

I'd missed the train from Goldens Bridge.

Homeless men in shabby jackets held out their hands as I walked east on 42nd Street. I imagined being someone who didn't understand their gestures, a stranger to impoverishment. I kicked up the blackened leaves that'd collected under the Tudor City overpass before arriving at First Avenue, where the UN building loomed like a giant credit card. All it'd take was a little push. Standing a few feet to my right, a man in a black overcoat held up a tattered cardboard sign that read "Are you kidding me?" When he smiled, his teeth flashed inside his massive beard, a long waterfall of graying rust like the needles of a dead Christmas tree. Cars on the avenue honked. Passengers pointed at us as if they'd discovered an important clue. The man lifted his sign higher and higher in response. He jumped up and down.

"What does it mean?" I asked.

"What?" he said, slightly out of breath.

"Your sign. What are you protesting?"

"The slaughter of children," he said indignantly.

"What children?"

"Jesus, read the newspaper, asshole."

When the light changed, I went over to the river. A trash barge heaped with silver metal scraps lazed downstream. I could see smoke rising from the runaway fires in Queens. There were so many now that I'd stopped questioning them. But the fires reminded me of my apartment and that I was probably running out of time. The sanitation buildings had a recharge area. The other option was to keep going. Maybe if I was lucky I'd end up on the Fresh Kills barge. The sky, a washed out watercolor, nearly gray, masked the promise of a beautiful morning, and I felt encouraged to walk south past the ambassadors maneuvering through checkpoints and the empty playgrounds below the FDR. On the sidewalk near the university hospital, a bewildered old couple were arguing. Their eyes were milky with cataracts. I carried them away from traffic and over to a woman in burgundy scrubs, who smiled and said, "I'll take it from here." I watched the three of them go inside. Life was an endless rebuke, and maybe the feelings weren't mine, but I was still the one feeling them. As I turned back to the avenue, a white van slowed to a stop in front of me. I'd seen the van before, in the periphery, or in memories, or maybe it was just the scene I was living in, I wasn't sure, it was impossible to know. A blunt, rectangular man jumped out of the back and swatted me inside.

"What the fuck?!" I shouted.

The driver was bald and wore diamond-studs in both ears. I yelled for him to stop the van but he didn't even grunt, he just stared at the traffic ahead, and eventually I surrendered to the experience. After a few hours on the highway, we made our way through a burned forest. There were many hundreds of black, decapitated stalks on slopes of ash, and the air was damp and heavy with smoke. I asked the men what'd happened, was it arson, but they didn't respond. The man in the passenger seat opened the glove box and slammed it shut just to hear the sound. Outside, the wreckage gave way to a clearing. Dead raccoons lying on the side of the road watched us through evacuated eyes. In the many times I'd imagined death, it'd never seemed so meaningless. A mile later, the driver took a winding road that led back toward the forest, but we passed trees that hadn't been burned. Their shadows swept into the van. Their branches scraped against the window. The forest floor crunched under the tires. We came to an iron gate entangled in leaves, which opened onto a horseshoe driveway. Several cars—an Escalade, a BMW, a Jaguar and three Teslas—were parked in front of a modern stone castle with a lawn so green it looked like it came from a factory. I was quickly rushed to the door and thrown into the velvet darkness inside.

I walked through a corridor and into a large hall. The door shut behind me and the lock clicked. I was in a large room filled with soft, warm light from gilded flush mounts that looked like oversized beetles clinging to the walls. All the windows had been papered over with thick tape, and couches in a neoclassical style were scattered throughout the room with odd intention—some stood back to back, others perpendicular. The floor was so heavily polished that I could see myself reflected as I stepped across it. I was like a kidnapped god traversing a private sea. I didn't notice the ceiling until I sat down because it was so far away, it must've been twenty feet high and featured a mural painted in a classical manner, with winged seraphim blowing horns and iridescent clouds wreathed around a familiar, white-bearded protagonist. It was a facile tableau but also painful for me, how many images had been created in the service of a god who had rendered man in *his* image, because I was born from the same impulse, but whether it was a shrewd admission or stunning blind spot, I could never tell. I suppose it was difficult to reckon with since it'd been going on for many hundreds of years. Like me, the painting held an elusive function—even if I didn't understand it, I wished they did. Though what human child couldn't say the same.

Guests began to filter into the room, men and women in black finery, all of them white and in their fifties. They talked and laughed in an exaggerated manner, to mask some shared anxiety, and they became quiet when they saw me, as if I were an actor and had just taken the stage. I approached them nervously, as I was supposed to, and held out my hand. Some of them retreated, there were about ten in all, until a woman in a loose black gown called out, "Jonathan?"

A man with an immaculate silver beard stepped forward. His eyes were singed brown, and his shoulders seemed to overwhelm him, as if he were bearing a terrible weight.

"Yes, of course, Marlena," he said.

The others tittered and clapped. The man motioned for me to follow. He led me to the corner and the others clustered around us. Instead of kissing me or reaching for my pulse, the man unbelted his black trousers and began to gently stroke himself. Anxiously I waited for him to take my wrist, but he didn't, he just stared at me with contempt, and I watched as his hand moved up and down and his face stuttered between threats of pleasure and shame.

The other guests were settling onto different couches and untangling from their clothes. The woman in the black gown was already leaned against the curved back of a chaise lounge with her dress hitched above her waist and her white lace underwear wrapped around her ankle boot like a manacle. Without taking her eyes off me, she swiped two fingers between her legs in fervent halos. I assumed that was my signal, but when I approached she made no effort to touch me, only herself, and more urgently, as if she were trying to erase an errant stain that wouldn't come out. Softly she moaned, they were all moaning now, quietly to themselves, and I approached each one of them on whatever couch they'd claimed—but no one laid a hand on me, they only stared at me with rapture and hostility, as if they were all part of the same machine, a machine of identical pleasures and powers, a system I was supposed to facilitate but could never be a part of. Maybe I was exhausted, maybe I was programmed to react the way I did—in any case, I raced for the door and ran into the night.

I thrashed through the woods, tripping over branches and hacking through weeds. The darkness was suffocating. The cold air blunted the scrape of the thorns. I stumbled from the brush into a coppice and dodged all manner of trees. After an hour I came to the clearing we'd passed on the way in, and then the burned-down forest. The charred trees stood in disheveled rows like massacred soldiers and I sat down on the ash to rest. There was no one coming for me, and I wasn't going anywhere anymore. Above, the night sky seemed to be made of incalculable black threads, and behind the threads burned the whitest, hottest light imaginable, brighter and more powerful than the sun, and whatever light leaked through were stars. Each star received a name and a part in a story—of safe harbor, the detonating flower of the universe, a poet's silver ash—and they became trapped in the image of their reflections, caught between two mirrors, until they burst and died, not knowing.

Acknowledgments

There are many people entangled in this book, who helped shape these stories and create the object. I want to thank Jamie Andersson, Adam Reed, Coryn Brown, Jocelyn Meinhardt, Yasmine Alwan, Genya Turovskaya, Caren Beilin, Kathleen Heil, Jen Hayashida, Gabriel Louis, Ashley Mayne, Andrea Lawlor, Harris Lahti, and Rav Grewal-Kök for their friendship, generosity, patience, humor, and intellect. An extra note of gratitude for Rav, who provided repeated and much-needed course corrections. To Lynne Tillman, I'm forever grateful for your unrivaled brilliance, your creativity, and your support. Thank you to the editors and magazines that published versions of these stories, including Michelle King at *Joyland*, Caitlin Palmer at *Fugue*, Rae Cline at *Eckleburg Review*, Ryan Ridge at *Juked*, and especially Mónica de la Torre at *Bomb*, who bought me years of unreasonable confidence. To Ariana Den Bleyker, Keith Powell and everyone at ELJ Editions, you are a gift. Thank you for sharing these stories with the world. Thank you to Paul Chan for seeing what I see and expressing it with such powerful madness on the cover of the book. And an endless waterfall of thank you to Bianca and Siobhan—I am nothing without you, I am everything because of you, your love and support sustain me.

About the Author

Trey Sager is the author of *Fires of Siberia*, *Dear Failures*, *O New York*, and the *Weeds*. His writing appears in *Bomb*, *Joyland*, the *Chicago Review*, the *Boston Review*, the *Poker*, *Juked*, *Fugue* and other journals. For many years he served as fiction editor for *Fence* magazine. Currently, he's working on a memoir about growing up with deaf oralist parents. He lives in New York City with his wife and daughter.

www.ingramcontent.com/pod-product-compliance
Lightning Source LLC
Chambersburg PA
CBHW032253070726

47590CB00016B/2614